Star Man's Son

※

andre norton

FAWCETT CREST · NEW YORK

STAR MAN'S SON

THIS BOOK CONTAINS THE COMPLETE TEXT OF
THE ORIGINAL HARDCOVER EDITION.

Published by Fawcett Crest Books, a unit of CBS Publica-
tions, the Consumer Publishing Division of CBS Inc. by ar-
rangement with Harcourt Brace, Jovanovich, Inc.

Copyright © 1952 by Harcourt Brace, Jovanovich, Inc.

ISBN: 0-449-23614-5

Printed in the United States of America

10 9 8 7 6 5 4 3 2 1

Star Man's Son

1

A Thief by Night

A NIGHT MIST WHICH WAS almost fog-thick still wrapped most of the Eyrie in a cottony curtain. Beads of moisture gathered on the watcher's bare arms and hide jerkin. He licked the wetness from his lips. But he made no move toward shelter, just as he had not during any of the long black hours behind him.

Hot anger had brought him up on this broken rock point above the village of his tribe. And something which was very close to real heartbreak kept him there. He propped a pointed chin—strong, cleft and stubborn—on the palm of a grimy hand and tried to pick out the buildings which made straight angles in the mist below.

Right before him, of course, was the Star Hall. And as he studied its rough stone walls, his lips drew tight in what was almost a noiseless snarl. To be one of the Star Men, honored by all the tribe, consecrated to the gathering and treasuring of knowledge, to the breaking of new trails and the exploration of lost lands—he, Fors of the Puma Clan, had never dreamed of any other life. Up until the hour of the Council Fire last night he had kept on

7

hoping that he would be given the right to enter the Hall. But he had been a child and a fool to so hope when all the signs had read just the opposite. For five years he had been passed over at the choosing of youths as if he did not exist. Why then should his merits suddenly become diamond-bright on the sixth occasion?

Only—his head dropped and his teeth clenched. Only—this was the last year—the very last year for him. Next year he would be over the age limit allowed a novice. When he was passed over last night—

Maybe—if his father had come back from the last exploring venture— If he himself didn't bear the stigma so plainly— His fingers clutched the thick hair on his head, tugging painfully as if he would have it all out by the roots. His hair was the worst! They might have forgotten about his night sight and too-keen hearing. He could have concealed those as soon as he learned how wrong it was to be different. But he could not hide the color of his close-cropped hair. And that had damned him from the day his father had brought him here. Other men had brown or black, or, at the worst, sun-bleached yellow, covering their heads. He had silver white, which showed to all men that he was a mutant, different from the rest of his clan. Mutant! Mutant!

For more than two hundred years—ever since the black days of chaos following the Great Blow-up, the atomic war—that cry had been enough to condemn without trial. Fear caused it, the strong, instinctive fear of the whole race for anyone cursed with a different physique or unusual powers.

Ugly tales were told of what had happened to the mutants, those unfortunates born in the first year after the Blow-up. Some tribes had taken drastic steps in those days to see that the strain of human—or almost human—lineage be kept pure.

Here in the Eyrie, far apart from the infection of the bombed sectors, mutation had been almost unknown. But he, Fors, had Plains' blood—tainted, unclean—and, since he could remember at all, he had never been allowed to put that fact from him.

While his father had lived it had not been so bad. The other children had yelled at him and there had been fights. But somehow, his father's confidence in him had made even that seem natural. And in the evenings, when they had shut out the rest of the Eyrie, there had been long hours of learning to read and write, to map and observe, the lore of the high trails and the low. Even among the Star Men his father had been a master instructor. And never had it appeared doubtful to Langdon that his only son Fors would follow him into the Star Hall.

So even after his father had failed to return from a trip to the lowlands, Fors had been confident of the future. He had made his weapons, the long bow now lying beside him, the short stabbing sword, the hunting knife—all with his own hands according to the Law. He had learned the trails and had found Lura, his great hunting cat—thus fulfilling all the conditions for the Choosing. For five years he had come to the Fire each season, with diminishing hope to be sure, and each time to be ignored as if he did not exist. And now he was too old to try again.

Tomorrow—no, today—he would have to lay aside his weapons and obey the dictates of the Council. Their verdict would be that he live on sufferance—which was probably all a mutant could expect—as a worker in one of the cave-sheltered Hydro farms.

No more schooling, no fifteen or twenty years of roving the lowlands, with further honored years to look forward to as an instructor and guardian of knowledge—a Star Man, explorer of the wilderness existing in the land where the Great Blow-up had made a world hostile to man. He would have no part in tracing the old cities where forgotten knowledge might be discovered and brought back to the Eyrie, in mapping roads and trails, helping to bring light out of darkness. He couldn't surrender that dream to the will of the Council!

A low questioning sound came out of the dark and absently he answered with an assenting thought. A shadow detached itself from a jumble of rocks and crept on velvet feet, soft belly fur dragging on the moss, to him. Then a furred shoulder almost as wide as his own nudged against him and he dropped a hand to scratch behind pricked ears. Lura was impatient. All the wild scents of the woods were rich in her widened nostrils and she wanted to be on the trail. His hand on her head was a restraint she half resented.

Lura loved freedom. What service she gave was of her own choosing, after the manner of her kind. He had been so proud two years ago when the most beautifully marked kitten of Kanda's last litter had shown such a preference for his company. One day Jarl himself—the Star Captain—had commented on it. How that had raised Fors' hopes—but nothing had come of the incident. Only Lura herself. He rubbed his hot cheek against the furry head raised to his. She made again the little questioning sound deep in her throat. She knew his unhappiness.

There was no sign of sunrise. Instead black clouds were gathering above the bald top of the Big Knob. It would be a stormy day and those below would keep within shelter. The moisture of the mist had become a drizzle and Lura was manifestly angry at his stubbornness in not going indoors. But if he went into any building of the Eyrie now it would be in surrender—a surrender to the loss of the life he had been born to lead, a surrender to all the whispers, the badge of shameful failure, to the stigma of being mutant—not as other men. And he could not do that—he couldn't!

If Langdon had stood before the Council last night—

Langdon! He could remember his father so vividly, the tall strong body, the high-held head with its bright, restless, seeking eyes above a tight mouth and sharp jaw.

Only— Langdon's hair had been safely dark. It was from his unknown Plainswoman mother that Fors had that too fair hair which branded him as one apart.

Langdon's shoulder bag with its star badge hung now in the treasure room of the Star Hall. It had been found with his battered body on the site of his last battle. A fight with the Beast Things seldom ended in victory for the mountaineers.

He had been on the track of a lost city when he had been killed. Not a "blue city," still forbidden to men if they wished to live, but a safe place without radiation which could be looted for the advantage of the Eyrie. For the hundredth time Fors wondered if his father's theory concerning the tattered bit of map was true—if a safe city did lie somewhere to the north on the edge of a great lake, ready and waiting for the man lucky and reckless enough to search it out.

"Ready and waiting—" Fors repeated the words aloud. Then his hand closed almost viciously on Lura's fur. She growled warningly at his roughness, but he did not hear her.

Why—the answer had been before him all along! Perhaps five years ago he could not have tried it—perhaps this eternal waiting and disappointment had been for the best after all. Because now he was ready—he knew it! His strength and the ability to use it, his knowledge and his wits were all ready.

No light yet showed below. The clouds were prolonging the night. But his time of grace was short, he would have to move fast! The bow, the filled quiver, the sword, were hidden between two rocks. Lura crawled in beside them to wait, his unspoken suggestion agreeing with her own desires.

Fors crept down the twisted trail to the Eyrie and made for the back of the Star Hall. The bunks of the Star Men on duty were all in the forepart of the house, the storage room was almost directly before him. And luck was favoring him as it never had before for the heavy shutter was not bolted or even completely closed as his exploring fingers discovered. After all—no one had ever dreamed of invading the Star Hall unasked.

Moving as noiselessly as Lura he swung over the high sill and stood breathing in a sort of light flutter. To the ordinary man of the Eyrie the room would have been almost pitch dark. But, for once, Fors' mutant night sight was an aid. He could see the long table, the benches, without difficulty, make out the line of pouches hanging on the far wall. These were his goal. His hand closed unerringly on one he had helped to pack many times. But when he lifted it from its hook he detached the gleaming bit of metal pinned to its strap.

To his father's papers and belongings he might prove some shadowy claim. But to that Star he had no right. His lips twisted in a bitter grimace as he laid the badge down on the edge of the long table before clambering back into the grayness of the outer world.

Now that the pouch swung from his shoulder he went openly to the storage house and selected a light blanket, a hunter's canteen and a bag of traveler's corn kept in readiness there. Then, reclaiming his weapons and the impatient Lura, he started off—not toward the narrow mountain valleys where all of his hunting had been done, but down toward the forbidden plains. A chill born of excitement rather than the bite of the rising wind roughened his skin, but his step was sure and confident as he hunted out the path blazed by Langdon more than ten years before, a path which was not overlooked by any station of the outpost guards.

Many times around the evening fires had the men of the Eyrie discussed the plains below and the strange world which had felt the force of the Great Blow-up and been turned into an alien, poisonous trap for any human not knowing its ways. Why, in the past twenty years even the Star Men had mapped only four cities, and one of those was "blue" and so must be avoided.

They knew the traditions of the old times. But, Langdon had always insisted even while he was repeating the stories to Fors, they could not judge how much of this information had been warped and distorted by time. How could they be sure that they were of the same race as those who had lived before the Blow-up? The radiation sickness, which had cut the number of survivors in the Eyrie to less than half two years after the war, might well have altered the future generations. Certainly the misshapen Beast Things must once have had a human origin though that was difficult for any who saw them now to believe. But they clung to the old cities and there the worst of the change took place.

The men of the Eyrie had records to prove that their forefathers had been a small band of technicians and scientists engaged in some secret research, cut off from a world which disappeared so quickly. But there were the Plainsmen of the wide grasslands, also free from the taint of the beast, who had survived and now roamed with their herds.

And there might be others.

Who had started the atomic war was unknown. Fors had once seen an old book containing jotted fragments of messages which had come out of the air through machines during a single horrible day. And these broken messages only babbled of the death of a world.

But that was all the men of the mountains knew of the last war. And while they fought ceaselessly to keep alive the old skills and learning there was so much, so very much, they no longer understood. They had old maps with pink and green, blue and yellow patches all carefully marked. But the pink and green, blue and yellow areas had had no defense against fire and death from the air and so had ceased to be. Only now could men, venturing out from their pockets of safety into the unknown, bring back bits of knowledge which they might piece together into history.

Somewhere within a mile or so of the trail he had chosen, Fors knew that there was a section of pre-Blow-up road. And that might be followed by the cautious for about a day's journey north. He had seen and handled the various trophies brought back by his father and his father's comrades, but he had never actually traveled the old roads or sniffed the air of the lowlands for himself. His pace quickened to a lope and he did not even feel the steady pour of the rain which streamed across his body plastering even his blanket to him. Lura protested with every leap she made to keep pace with him, but she did not go back. The excitement which drew him on at such an unwary speed had spread to the always sensitive mind of the great cat and she made her way through the underbrush with sinuous ease.

The old road was almost a disappointment when he stumbled out upon it. Once it must have had a smooth surface, but time, disuse, and the spreading greedy force of wild vegetation had seamed and broken it. Nevertheless it was a marvel to be examined closely by one who had never seen such footing before. Men had ridden on it once encased in machines. Fors knew that, he had seen pictures of such machines, but their fashioning was now a mystery. The men of the Eyrie knew facts about them, painfully dug out of the old books brought back from city lootings, but the materials and fuels for their production were now beyond hope of obtaining.

Lura did not like the roadway. She tried it with a cautious paw, sniffed at the upturned edge of a block, and went back to firm ground. But Fors stepped out on it boldly, walking the path of the Old Ones even when it would have been easier to take to the bush. It gave him an odd feeling of power to tread so. This stuff beneath his hide boots had been fashioned by those of his race who had been wiser and stronger and more learned. It was up to those of his breed to regain that lost wisdom.

"Ho, Lura!"

The cat paused at his exultant call and swung the dark brown mask of her face toward him. Then she meowed plaintively, conveying the thought that she was being greatly misused by this excursion into the dampness of an exceedingly unpleasant day.

She was beautiful indeed. Fors' feeling of good will and happiness grew within him as he watched her. Since he had left the last step of the mountain trail he had felt a curious sense of freedom and for the first time in his life he did not care about the color of his hair or feel that he must be inferior to the others of the clan. He had all his father had taught him well in mind, and in the pouch swinging at his side his father's greatest secret. He had a long bow no other youth of his age could string, a bow of his own making. His sword was sharp and balanced to suit his hand alone. There was all the lower world before him and the best of companions to match his steps.

Lura licked at her wet fur and Fors caught a flash of—was it her thoughts or just emotion? None of the Eyrie dwellers had ever been able to decide how the great cats were able to communicate with the men they chose to honor with their company. Once there had been dogs to run with man— Fors had read of them. But the strange radiation sickness had been fatal to the dogs of the Eyrie and their breed had died out forever.

Because of that same plague the cats had changed. Small domestic animals of untamable independence had produced larger offspring with even quicker minds and greater strength. Mating with wild felines from the tainted plains had established the new mutation. The creature which now rubbed against Fors was the size of a mountain lion of pre-Blow-up days, but her thick fur was of a deep shade of cream, darkening on head, legs, and tail to a chocolate brown—after the coloring set by a Siamese ancestor first brought into the mountains by the wife of a research engineer. Her eyes were the deep sapphire blue of a true gem, but her claws were cruelly sharp and she was a master hunter.

That taste possessed her now as she drew Fors' attention to a patch of moist ground where the slot of a deer was deep marked. The trail was fresh—even as he studied it a bit of sand tumbled from the top into the hollow of the mark. Deer meat was good and he had few supplies. It might be worth turning aside. He need not speak to Lura—she knew his decision and was off on the trail at once. He padded after her with the noiseless woods walk he had learned so long before that he could not remember the lessons.

The trail led off at a right angle from the remains of the old road, across the tumbled line of a wall where old bricks protruded at crazy points from heaped earth and brush. Water from leaves and branches doused both hunters, gluing Fors' homespun leggings to his legs and squeezing into his boots.

He was puzzled. By the signs, the deer had been fleeing for its life and yet whatever menaced it had left no trace. But Fors was not afraid. He had never met any living thing, man or animal, which could stand against the force of his steel-tipped arrows or which he would have hesitated to face, short sword in hand.

Between the men of the mountains and the roving Plainsmen there was a truce. The Star Men often lived for periods of time in the skin-walled tents of the herders, exchanging knowledge of far places with those eternal wanderers. And his father had taken a wife among the outlanders. Of course, there was war to the death between the humankind and the Beast Things which skulked in the city ruins. But the latter had never been known to venture far from their dank, evil-smelling burrows in the shattered buildings, and certainly one need not fear meeting with them in this sort of open country! So he followed the trail with a certain reckless disregard.

The trail ended suddenly on the lip of a small gully. Some ten feet or so below, a stream—swollen by the rain—frothed around green-grown rocks. Lura was on her belly, pulling her body forward along the rim of the ravine. Fors dropped down and inched behind a bush. He knew better than to interfere with her skillful approach.

When the tip of her brown tail quivered he watched for a trembling of Lura's flat flanks which would signalize her spring. But instead the tail suddenly bristled and the shoulders hunched as if to put a brake upon muscles already tensed. He caught her message of bewilderment, of disgust and, yes, of fear.

He knew that he had better eyesight than almost all of the Eyrie men, that had been proved many times. But what had stopped Lura in her tracks was gone. True, upstream a bush still swayed as if something had just pushed past it. But the sound of the water covered any noise and although he strained—there was nothing to see.

Lura's ears lay flat against her skull and her eyes were slits of blazing rage. But beneath the rage Fors grasped another emotion—almost fear. The big cat had come across something strange and therefore to be considered with suspicion. Aroused by her message Fors lowered himself over the edge of the gully. Lura made no attempt to stop him. Whatever had troubled her was gone, but he was determined to see what traces it might have left in its passing.

The greenish stones of the river bank were sleek and slippery with spray, and twice he had to catch hurriedly at bushes to keep from falling into the stream. He got to his hands and knees to move across one rock and then he was at the edge of the bush which had fluttered.

A red pool, sticky but already being diluted by the rain and the spray, filled a clay hollow. He tasted it with the aid of a finger. Blood. Probably that of the deer they had been following.

Then, just beyond, he saw the spoor of the hunter that had brought it down. It was stamped boldly into the clay, deeply as if the creature that made it had balanced for a moment under a weight, perhaps the body of the deer. And it was too clear to mistake the outline—the print of a naked foot.

No man of the Eyrie, no Plainsman had left that track! It was narrow and the same width from heel to toe—as if the thing which had left it was completely flat-footed. The toes were much too long and skeleton-thin. Beyond their tips were indentations of—not nails—but what must be real claws!

Fors' skin crawled. It was unhealthy—that was the word which came into his mind as he stared at the track. He was glad—and then ashamed of that same gladness— that he had not seen the hunter in person.

Lura pushed past him. She tasted the blood with a dainty tongue and then lapped it once or twice before she came on to inspect his find. Again flattened ears and wrinkled, snarling lips gave voice to her opinion of the vanished hunter. Fors strung his bow for action. For the first time the chill of the day struck him. He shivered as a flood of water spouted at him over the rocks.

With more caution they went back up the slope. Lura showed no inclination to follow any trail the unknown hunter might have left and Fors did not suggest it to her. This wild world was Lura's real home and more than once the life of a Star Man had depended upon the instincts of his hunting cat. If Lura saw no reason to risk her skin downriver, he would abide by her choice.

They came back to the road. But now Fors used hunting craft and the trail-covering tricks which normally one kept only for the environs of a ruined city—those haunted places where death still lay in wait to strike down the unwary. It had stopped raining but the clouds did not lift.

Toward noon he brought down a fat bird Lura flushed out of a tangle of brush and they shared the raw flesh of the fowl equally.

It was close to dusk, a shadow time coming early because of the storm, when they came out upon a hill above the dead village the old road served.

2

Into the Midst of Yesterday

EVEN IN THE PRE-BLOW-UP days when it had been lived
in, the town must have been neither large nor impressive.
But to Fors, who had never before seen any buildings but
those of the Eyrie, it was utterly strange and even a bit
frightening. The wild vegetation had made its claim and
moldering houses were now only lumps under the green-
ery. One water-worn pier at the edge of the river which
divided the town marked a bridge long since fallen away.

Fors hesitated on the heights above for several long
minutes. There was a forbidding quality in that tangled
wilderness below, a sort of moldy rankness rising on the
evening wind from the hollow which cupped the ruins.
Wind, storm and wild animals had had their way there
too long.

On the road to one side was a heap of rusted metal
which he thought must be the remains of a car such as
the men of the old days had used for transportation. Even
then it must have been an old one. Because just before the
Blow-up they had perfected another type, powered by
atom engines. Sometimes Star Men had found those al-

most intact. He skirted the wreckage and, keeping to the thread of battered road, went down into the town.

Lura trotted beside him, her head high as she tested each passing breeze for scent. Quail took flight into the tall grass and somewhere a cock pheasant called. Twice the scut of a rabbit showed white and clear against the green.

There were flowers in that tangle, defending themselves with hooked thorns, the running vines which bore them looped and relooped into barriers he could not crash through. And all at once the setting sun broke between cloud lines to bring their scarlet petals into angry life. Insects chirped in the grass. The storm was over.

The travelers pushed through into an open space bordered on all sides by crumbling mounds of buildings. From somewhere came the sound of water and Fors beat a path through the rank shrubbery to where a trickle of a stream fed a man-made basin.

In the lowlands water must always be suspect—he knew that. But the clear stream before him was much more appetizing than the musty stuff which had sloshed all day in the canteen at his belt. Lura lapped it unafraid, shaking her head to free her whiskers from stray drops. So he dared to cup up a palmful and sip it gingerly.

The pool lay directly before a freak formation of rocks which might have once been heaped up to suggest a cave. And the mat of leaves which had collected inside there was dry. He crept in. Surely there would be no danger in camping here. One never slept in any of the old houses, of course. There was no way of telling whether the ghosts of ancient disease still lingered in their rottenness. Men had died from that carelessness. But here— In among the leaves he saw white bones. Some other hunter—a four-footed one—had already dined.

Fors kicked out the refuse and went prospecting for wood not too sodden to burn. There were places in and among the clustered rocks where winds had piled branches and he returned to the cave with one, then two, and finally three armloads, which he piled within reaching distance.

Out in the plains fire could be an enemy as well as a friend. A carelessly tended blaze in the wide grasslands might start one of the oceans of flame which would run for miles driving all living things before it. And in an enemy's country it was instant betrayal. So even when he had his small circle of sticks in place Fors hesitated, flint and steel in hand. There was the mysterious hunter—what if he were lurking now in the maze of the ruined town?

Yet both he and Lura were chilled and soaked by the rain. To sleep cold might mean illness to come. And, while he could stomach raw meat when he had to, he relished it broiled much more. In the end it was the thought of the meat which won over his caution, but even when a thread of flame arose from the center of his wheel of sticks, his hand still hovered ready to put it out. Then Lura came up to watch the flames and he knew that she would not be so at her ease if any danger threatened. Lura's eyes and nose were both infinitely better than his own.

Later, simply by freezing into a hunter's immobility by the pool, he was able to knock over three rabbits. Giving Lura two, he skinned and broiled the third. The setting sun was red and by the old signs he could hope for a clear day tomorrow. He licked his fingers, dabbled them in the water, and wiped them on a tuft of grass. Then for the first time that day he opened the pouch he had stolen before the dawn.

He knew what was inside, but this was the first time in years that he held in his hand again the sheaf of brittle old papers and read the words which had been carefully traced across them in his father's small, even script. Yes—he was humming a broken little tune—it *was* here, the scrap of map his father had treasured so—the one which showed the city to the north, a city which his father had hoped was safe and yet large enough to yield rich loot for the Eyrie.

But it was not easy to read his father's cryptic notes. Langdon had made them for his own use and Fors could only guess at the meaning of such directions as "snake river to the west of barrens," "Northeast of the wide forest" and all the rest. Landmarks on the old maps were now gone, or else so altered by time that a man might pass a turning point and never know it. As Fors frowned over the scrap which had led his father to his death he began to realize a little of the enormity of the task before him. Why, he didn't even know all the safe trails which had been blazed by the Star Men through the years, except by hearsay. And if he became lost—

His fingers tightened around the roll of precious papers. Lost in the lowlands! To wander off the trails—!

Silky fur pressed against him and a round head butted his ribs. Lura had caught that sudden nip of fear and was answering it in her own way. Fors' lungs filled slowly. The humid air of the lowlands lacked the keen bite of the mountain winds. But he was free and he was a man. To return to the Eyrie was to acknowledge defeat. What if he did lose himself down here? There was a whole wide land to make his own! Why, he could go on and on across it until he reached the salt sea which tradition said lay at the rim of the world. This whole land was his for the exploring!

He delved deeper into the bag on his knee. Besides the notes and the torn map he found the compass he had hoped would be there, a small wooden case containing pencils, a package of bandages and wound salve, two small surgical knives, and a roughly fashioned notebook—the daily record of the Star Man. But to his vast disappointment the entries there were merely a record of distances. On impulse he set down on one of the blank pages an account of his own day's travel, trying to make a drawing of the strange footprint. Then he repacked the pouch.

Lura stretched out on the leaf bed and he flopped down beside her, pulling the blanket over them both. It was twilight now. He pushed the sticks in toward the center of the fire so that the unburnt ends would be consumed. The soft rumble of the cat's purr as she washed her paws, biting at the spaces between her claws, made his eyes heavy. He flung an arm over her back and she favored him with a lick of her tongue. The rasp of it across his skin was the last thing he clearly remembered.

There were birds in the morning, a whole flock of them, and they did not approve of Lura. Their scolding cries brought Fors awake. He rubbed his eyes and looked out groggily at a gray world. Lura sat in the mouth of the cave, paying no attention to the chorus over her head. She yawned and looked back at Fors with some impatience.

He dragged himself out to join her and pulled off his roughly dried clothes before bathing in the pool. It was cold enough to set him sputtering and Lura withdrew to a safe distance. The birds flew away in a black flock. Fors dressed, lacing up his sleeveless jerkin and fastening his boots and belt with extra care.

A more experienced explorer would not have wasted time on the forgotten town. Long ago any useful loot it might have once contained had either been taken away or had moldered into rubbish. But it was the first dead place Fors had seen and he could not leave it without some examination. He followed the road around the square. Only one building still stood unharmed enough to allow entrance. Its stone walls were rank with ivy and moss and its empty windows blind. He shuffled through the dried leaves and grass which masked the broad flight of steps leading to its wide door.

There was the whir of disturbed grasshoppers in the leaves, a wasp sang past. Lura pawed at something which lay just within the doorway. It rolled away into the dusk of the interior and they followed. Fors stopped to trace with an inquiring finger the letters on a bronze plate.

"First National Bank of Glentown."

He read the words aloud and they echoed hollowly down the long room, through the empty cage-like booths along the wall.

"First National Bank," he repeated. What was a bank? He had only a vague idea—some sort of a storage place. And this dead town must be Glentown—or once it had been Glentown.

Lura had found again her round toy and was batting it along the cracked flooring. It skidded to strike the base of one of the cages just in front of Fors. Round eyeholes stared up at him accusingly from a half-crushed skull. He stooped and picked it up to set it on the stone shelf. Dust arose in a thick puff. A pile of coins spun and jingled in all directions, their metallic tinkle clear.

There were lots of the coins here, all along the shelves behind the cage fronts. He scooped up handfuls and sent them rolling to amuse Lura. But they had no value. A piece of good, rust-proof steel would be worth the taking—not these. The darkness of the place began to oppress him and no matter which way he turned he thought he could feel the gaze of that empty skull. He left, calling Lura to follow.

There was a dankness in the heart of this town, the air here had the faint corruption of ancient decay, mixed with the fresher scent of rotting wood and moldering vegetation. He wrinkled his nose against it and pushed on down a choked street, climbing over piles of rubble, heading toward the river. That stream had to be crossed some way if he were to travel straight to the goal his father had mapped. It would be easy for him to swim the thick brownish water, still roily from the storm, but he knew that Lura would not willingly venture in and he was certainly not going to leave her behind.

Fors struck out east along the bank above the flood. A

raft of some sort would be the answer, but he would have to get away from the ruins before he could find trees. And he chafed at the loss of time.

There was a sun today, climbing up, striking specks of light from the water. By turning his head he could still see the foothills and, behind them, the blueish heights down which he had come twenty-four hours before. But he glanced back only once, his attention was all for the river now.

Half an hour later he came across a find which saved him hours of back-breaking labor. A sharp break in the bank outlined a narrow cove where the river rose during the spring freshets. Now it was half choked with drift, from big logs to delicate, sunbleached twigs he could snap between his fingers. He had only to pick and choose.

By the end of the morning he had a raft, crude and certainly not intended for a long voyage, but it should serve to float them across. Lura had her objections to the foolishness of trusting to such a crazy woven platform. But, when Fors refused to stay safely ashore, she pulled herself aboard it, one cautious paw testing each step before she put her full weight upon it. And in the exact middle she squatted down with a sigh as Fors leaned hard on his pole and pushed off.

The weird craft showed a tendency to spin around which he had to work against. And once his pole caught in a mud bank below and he was almost jerked off into the flood. But as the salty sweat stung across his lips and burned in his blistered palms he could see that the current, though taking them downstream, was slowly nudging them toward the opposite bank.

Sun rays reflected by the water made them both warm and thirsty, and Lura gave small meowing whines of self-pity all the rest of the hour. Still, she grew accustomed enough to the new mode of travel to sit up and watch keen-eyed when a fish rose to snap at a fly. Once they slipped past a mass of decayed wreckage which must have been the remains of a boat, and twice swept between abutments of long-vanished bridges. This had been a thickly settled territory before the Blow-up. Fors tried to imagine what it had looked like when the towns had been lived in, the roads had been busy with traffic, when there had been boats on the river—

Since the current was taking them in the general direction of the route eastward he did not struggle too quickly to reach the other side. But when a portion of their shaky raft suddenly broke off and started a separate voyage of its own, he realized that such carelessness might mean trouble and he worked with the pole to break the grip of the current and reach the shore. There were bluffs along the river, cutting off easy access to the level lands behind them and he watched anxiously for a cove or sandbank which would give them a fair landing.

He had to be satisfied with a very shallow notch where a landslide had brought down a section of the bank containing two trees which now formed a partial barrier out from the shore. The raft, after much back-breaking labor on his part, caught against these, shivered against the pull of the water, and held. Lura did not wait, but was gone in a single leap to the solid footing of the tree trunks. Fors grabbed up his belongings and followed, none too soon, as the raft split and whirled around, shaking into pieces which were carried on.

A hard scramble up the greasy clay of the bank brought them into open country once more. Grass grew tall, bushes spread in dusty blotches across the land and there were thickets of saplings reclaiming the old fields. But here the wild had not altogether conquered land tamed by centuries of the plow and the reaper.

Lura let him know that it had been too long since their last meal and she intended to do something about supplies. She set off across the faint boundaries of the old fields with grim purpose in every line of her graceful feline body. Grouse scuttled from underfoot and there were rabbits everywhere, but she disdained to notice such small game, pushing on, with Fors half a field behind her, toward a slope which was crowned with a growth of trees, almost a full wood.

Halfway up she paused, the tip of her tail quivered, the red rosette of her tongue showed briefly between her teeth. Then she was gone again, fading away into the tall grass as silently and effortlessly as the breeze might pass. Fors stepped back into the shade of the nearest tree. This was Lura's hunt and he must leave it to her.

He looked out over the waving grass. It seemed to be some form of stunted grain, not yet quite ripe, for it had a seed head forming. The sky was blue with small white clouds drifting across it as if the storm winds had never torn them, although at his feet lay a branch splintered and broken by yesterday's wind.

A hoarse bellowing brought him out of his half dream, bow in hand. It was followed by the spitting squall which was Lura's war cry. Fors began to run up the slope toward the sound. But hunter's caution kept him to such shelter as the field afforded so he did not burst rashly out onto the scene of the combat.

Lura *had* tackled big game! He caught the sun flash on her tawny fur as she leaped away from an inert red-brown body just in time to escape the charge of a larger beast. A wild cow! And Lura had killed her calf!

Fors' arrow was already in the air. The cow bellowed again and tossed her wickedly horned head. She made a shambling run to the body of her calf, snorting in red rage. Then crimson froth puffed from her wide nostrils and she stumbled to her knees and fell on her side. Lura's round head shot up above a stand of thick grass and she moved out to the side of her prey. Fors came from the trees where he had taken cover. He would have echoed Lura's rasping purr had it been in his power. That arrow had gone straight and true to the mark he had set it.

It was a pity to have to waste all that meat. Enough to

keep three Eyrie families for a week lay there. He prodded the cow with a regretful toe before starting to butcher the calf.

He could, of course, try to jerk the meat. But he was unsure of the right method and he could not carry it with him anyway. So he contented himself with preparing what he could for the next few days while Lura, after feasting, slept under a bush, rousing now and then to snap at the gathering flies.

They made camp that night a field or two beyond the kill, in the corner of an old wall. Piles of fallen stones turned it into a position which could be defended if the need arose. But neither slept well. The fresh meat they had left behind drew night rovers. There was a scream or two which must have come from Lura's wild relatives and she growled in answer. Then in the early dawn there was a baying cry which Fors was unable to identify, woods learned as he was. But Lura went wild when she heard it, spitting in sheer hate, her fur rising stiff along her backbone.

It was early when Fors started on, striking across the open fields in the line set by his compass. Today he made no effort to keep cover or practice caution. He could see no menace in these waste fields. Why had there been all the talk back in the Eyrie about the danger in the lowlands? Of course, one did keep away from the "blue" patches where radiation still meant death even after all these years. And the Beast Things were always to be dreaded—had not Langdon died in their attack? But as far as the Star Men had been able to discover those nightmare creatures kept to the old cities and were not to be feared in the open. Surely these fields must be as safe for man as the mountain forests which encircled the Eyrie.

He took an easy curve and came out suddenly on a sight which brought him up—blinking. Here was a road—but such a road! The broken concrete was four times as wide as any he had seen—it had really been two roads running side by side with a stretch of earth between them, two wide roads running smoothly from one horizon to another.

But not two hundred yards from where he stood gaping, the road was choked with a tangle of rusting metal. A barrier of broken machines filled it from ditch to ditch. Fors approached it slowly. There was something about that monstrous wall which was forbidding—even though he knew that it had stood so for perhaps two hundred years. Black crickets jumped out of the weeds before him and a mouse flashed across a stretch of clear stone.

He rounded the jumble of wrecked machines. They must have been traveling along the road in a line when death had struck mysteriously, struck so that some of the machines had rammed others or wavered off to pile up in wild wreckage. Others stood solitary as if the dying driver had been able to bring them to a safe halt before he succumbed. Fors tried to pick out the outlines and associate what he saw with the ancient pictures. That—that was certainly a "tank," one of the moving fortresses of the Old Ones. Its gun still pointed defiantly to the sky. Two, four, five more he counted, and then gave up.

The column of machines stretched out in its forgotten disaster for almost a mile. Fors brushed along beside it in the waist-high weeds which bordered the road. He had a queer distaste for approaching the dead machines more closely, no desire to touch any of the bits of rusted metal. Here and there he saw one of the atom-powered vehicles, seeming almost intact. But they were dead too. All of it was dead, in a horrible way. He experienced a vague feeling of contamination from just walking beside the wreckage.

There were guns on the moving forts, guns which still swung ready, and there had been men, hundreds of men. He could see their white bones mixed with the rust and the debris driven in by years of wind and storm. Guns and men—where had they been going when the end came? And what was the end? There were none of the craters he had been told were to be found where bombs had fallen—just smashed machines and men, as if death had come as a mist or a wind.

Guns and men on the march—maybe to repel invaders. The book of air-borne messages treasured in the Eyrie had spoken once or twice of invaders coming from the sky—enemies who had struck with paralyzing swiftness. But something must have happened in turn to that enemy—or else why had the invaders not made the land their own? Probably the answer to that question would never be known.

Fors reached the end of the blasted column. But he kept on walking along the clean earth until he topped a rise and could no longer sight the end of a wasted war. Then he dared once more to walk the road of the Old Ones.

3

The Dark Hunter

ABOUT HALF A MILE FARTHER ON the shadow of a woodland swallowed up the road. Fors' heart lifted when he saw it. These open fields were strange to a mountain-born man but he felt at home in a thick cloak of trees such as the one before him now.

He was trying to remember the points on the big map which hung on the wall of the Star House, the map to which was added a tiny mark at the return of each roving explorer. This northern route crossed the wedge end of a portion of territory held loosely by Plainsmen. And the Plainsmen had horses—useless in the mountains and so untamed by his people—but very needful in this country of straight distances. To have a horse at his service now—

The cool of the woods lapped him in and he was at home at once, as was Lura. They padded on, their feet making but the faintest whisper of sound. It was a scent carried by a tiny puff of breeze which brought them up— Wood smoke!

Fors' thought met Lura's and agreed. She stood for a

long moment, testing the air with her keener nostrils, and then she turned aside, pushing between two birches. Fors scraped after her. The guiding puff of wind was gone, but he could smell something else. They were approaching a body of water—not running water or the sound of its passing would be heard.

There was a break in the foliage ahead. He saw Lura flatten herself out on a rock surface which was almost the same color as her own creamy hide, flatten and creep. And he hunkered down to follow her example, the gritty stone biting knees and hands as he wormed out beside her.

They were belly down on a spur of rock which overhung the surface of a woods-hemmed lake. Not far beyond a thread of stream trickled away and he could spot two islands, the nearest joined to the mainland by a series of stepping stones. On the shores of this islet crouched someone very busy over a cooking fire.

The stranger was no mountaineer, that was certain. In the first place his wide-shouldered, muscular bronze body was bare to the waist and at least five shades darker as to skin tint than the most deeply tanned of the Eyrie men. The hair on his round skull was black and tightly curled. He had strongly marked features with a wide-lipped mouth and flat cheekbones, his large dark eyes set far apart. His only clothing was a sort of breechclout kilt held in place by a wide belt from which hung the tassel-ornamented scabbard of a knife. The knife itself, close to eighteen inches of blue steel, flashed in his hand as he energetically cleaned a fresh-caught fish.

Stuck upright in the ground close to his shoulder were three short-shafted spears, a blanket of coarse reddish wool draped over the point of one. Smoke rose from the fire laid on a flat stone, but there was no indication as to whether the stranger had merely halted for a meal or had been camping on the islet.

As he worked the fisherman sang—a low, monotonous

chant, which, as he listened to it, affected Fors queerly, sending an odd shiver up his backbone. This was no Plainsman either. And Fors was just as sure that he was not spying on one of the Beast Things. The few mountaineer men who had survived a meeting with *them* had painted a far different picture—they were never to be associated with peaceful fishing and an intelligent, pleasant face.

This dark-skinned newcomer was of a different breed. Fors rested his chin on his folded arms and tried to deduce from the evidence this stranger's background—as was the duty of an explorer.

The lack of clothing now—that meant that he was accustomed to a warmer climate. Such an outfit could only be worn here before fall closed in. He had those spears and—yes—that was a bow lying with its quiver beyond. But it was much shorter than the one Fors carried and did not appear to be made of wood but from some dark substance which reflected light from the sun.

He must come from a land where his race was all-powerful and had nothing to fear for he camped in the open and sang while he cooked as if he did not care if he attracted attention. And yet he did this on an island, more easily defended from attack than the shore itself.

Just then the fisherman impaled the cleaned fish on a sharpened twig and set it to broil while he got to his feet and hurled a baited line back into the water. Fors blinked. The man on the island must tower a good four or five inches over the tallest of the Eyrie men and his thatch of upstanding hair could not account for more than two inches of that difference. As he stood there, still humming, his hands skillfully adjusting the fishing line, he presented a picture of strength and power which would daunt even a Beast Thing.

The odor of the fish carried. Lura made a faint slurruping sound as it reached them. Fors hesitated. Should he

hail the dark-skinned hunter, make the peace sign, and
try to establish friendly relations or—

That question was decided for him. A shout tore the
serene silence of the lake. The dark hunter moved—so
fast that Fors was left gasping. Spears, blanket, bow—and
the broiled fish—vanished with their owner. A bush
quivered and then was still. The fire burned—on a
deserted pebbled beach.

A second shout bore down wind, reinforced by a tram-
pling crash, and down to the edge of the lake trotted a
band of horses, mares mostly, each with a small foal running at her side. Urging them on were two riders, bent
nearly flat on the backs of their mounts to escape the low
sweeping branches of the trees. They herded the mares to
water and waited for them to drink.

Fors almost forgot the dark hunter. Horses! He had
seen pictures of them. But living horses! The age-old long-
ing of his race—to possess one of those for his own—
made a strange ache in his thigh muscles, as if he were
already mounted upon one of the sleek backs.

One of the horse guards had dismounted and was rubbing down the legs of his animal with handfuls of grass
pulled up from the bank. *He* was undoubtedly a Plainsman. His sleeveless jerkin laced across the chest was almost twin to the one Fors wore. But his leggings were of
hide and polished by hours of riding. He wore his hair
shoulder length as the sign of free birth and it was held
out of his eyes by a broad band on which was painted the
sign of his family clan and tribe. The long lance which was
the terrible weapon of the horsemen hung in its loops at
his saddle and in addition he wore at his belt the curved,
slashing sword which was the badge of his nation.

For the second time Fors wondered whether he should
make overtures. But that, too, was quickly answered. Out
of the trees came a second pair of riders, both older men.
One was a chief or sub chieftain of the Plainsmen, for the

metal badge in his headband had caught the sun. But the other—

Fors' body jerked as if an arrow had thudded home between his shoulder blades. And Lura, catching his dismay, voiced one of her noiseless snarls.

That was Jarl! But Jarl was the Star Captain—now exempt from travel in the lowlands. He had not been exploring for two years or more. It was his duty to remain at the Eyrie and portion out the tasks of other Star Men. But there he was, riding knee to knee with the Plainsman chief as if he were any apprentice rover. What had brought Jarl down to the lowlands against all rule and custom?

Fors winced—there was an answer to that. Never before had the sanctuary of the Star House been violated. His crime must have brought Jarl out of the hills. And if he, Fors, were captured— What would be the penalty for such a theft? He had no idea but his imagination could supply quite a few—all of them drastic. In the meantime he could only remain where he was and pray that he would not be detected before the herders moved.

Luckily most of the horses had drunk their fill and were turning away from the lake. Fors watched them longingly. With one of them to lend four feet and save his two, he could be well beyond Jarl's reach before the Star Captain knew of his presence. He had too great an opinion of Jarl's skill not to believe that the man from the Eyrie could cross his trail within a day or so.

The second herder urged the last mares away from the water while his companion mounted. But Jarl and the chief still sat talking and looking out idly across the lake. Fors silently endured the bites of flies which seemed to have accompanied the horses, but Lura growled again softly. She wanted to leave, knowing full well that if she did not want her trail followed it would not be. Fors could not hope for such results himself, so he hesitated until the cat's impatience or some change in the air current changed their luck as it carried Lura's scent down to the peaceful herd.

Within seconds there was wild confusion. Mares squealed, wild-eyed with fright for their foals, tramping up the bank and bursting between the riders—dashing ahead to get away from that dangerous place. The Plainsmen had been caught off guard. One was borne along with the rush, fighting to regain mastery of his own mount—the other could only ride after the rout.

Lance in hand the chief went after them. But Jarl remained where he was for a long moment, searching the shoreline of the lake with narrowed eyes. Fors flattened against the rock, sending a stern warning to Lura to do likewise. Fortunately Jarl was on the opposite side of the water and the Star Captain could not match the keen sight of his quarry. But how limited Jarl was in that respect he had no means of telling.

Hardly daring to draw the shallowest of breaths, cat and boy inched back. Jarl stayed, alert, watching. Then came the thunder of hoofs, just as Fors' boots struck earth. He was off at his best woods' pace, heading north, away from the camp which must lie somewhere on the other side of the lake. He wanted a horse, needed a horse, but not enough that he dared brave Jarl to get one. Fors had a very hearty respect for the abilities of the Star Captain.

As he sped away he wondered what the hunter on the island had done and whether he, too, was now putting some miles between himself and the Plains camp.

At least *he* had that broiled fish to take with him. Fors munched a handful of parched corn from his emergency rations as he trotted along and some shreds of dried meat, giving the rest to Lura who downed it in a single gulp. Half-ripe berries snatched from bushes as he passed were sauce of a sort. But there still remained a feeling of emptiness in his middle which grew with the lengthening shadows of the afternoon.

They had used the feeder stream of the lake as a guide, but the thinning of the trees around them now and the appearance of open patches where grass and bushes competed for life, suggested that the end of the wood was close. Fors paused and tried to plan. He was at home in the forest country and knew how to conceal his trail there. On the other hand, in the open, out in the once cultivated fields, one would make better time and be able to cover a good many miles before the daylight failed entirely. The hunters of the plains—if human—were mounted men and any pursuit would be easily seen. And there were plenty of the scattered clumps of trees and running tongues of brush to give him shelter in a pinch. He decided to venture out.

A brown animal with a black mask about its eyes surveyed him critically from a pile of rocks but was gone in a flash when Lura's head came out of a tall stand of grass. That was the only living thing they saw until they skirted the rotting timbers of a farmhouse, missing a tumble into the half exposed cellar only by chance.

A sound answered Fors' exclamation and hearing it his hand swept to the hilt of his sword. He skidded around, bare steel out. An ugly naked pink snout, still smeared with earth and slime, protruded from a tangle of brush, and the wicked tusks below it caught and held the light. Fors hurled pouch and bow from him and half crouched, waiting for that most dangerous of all rushes, the attack of a wild boar.

It came with all the deadly ferocity he had expected, the tusks slashing for his legs. He struck, but the creature dodged so that, though a red and dripping line leaped out along its head and shoulder, it was not sent kicking. It grunted loudly, and there came answers. Fors' mouth dried—he was facing a whole pack of swine!

Behind him was a pile of the collapsed timbers which had once been the wall of a small building, but they were pulpy with rot and they dipped dangerously toward the cellar. If he jumped for them he might well crash through.

From the bushes came a squall of rage and pain. The boar tossed its tusked head and blew foam. Its eyes in the black-and-white spotted face were red and evil. Another squeal came from the herd and this time it was followed by an answering snarl. Fors loosed a thankful breath.

Lura was keeping the herd occupied. Under her ripping claws the younger and weaker ones would certainly break and scatter. But not this old leader. It was wily and there were scars and bare patches enough on the hide to mark it victor in other battles. It had always won before so it was confident now. And— The charge came again!

Fors leaped to the left, slashing down as he moved out of danger. That stroke cut across the grinning devil's mask of the boar, chopping off an ear and shearing the sight out of one red eye. It shook its head, sending a spray of blood flying, and squealed in rage and pain. Under the prod of pain it lost its cunning, wishing now only to tusk and trample the dancing figure before it—to root the life of the enemy away—

As Fors saw the heavy shoulders tense he took a step backward, groping for firm footing on which to maneuver. And in so doing he nearly lost the fight. His heel caught and was held as if a trap had snapped on it. He was still trying to pull loose as the boar charged for the third time.

And that pull unbalanced him so that he fell forward almost on top of the mad creature. There was a red dagger of pain across his leg and a foul stench filled his nostrils. He stabbed wildly, and felt his steel strike bone and slip deep beneath the mangy hide. Blood fountained over both of them and then the sword was wrenched from Fors' blood-slippery hand as the boar pulled away. It staggered out into the full sunlight and fell heavily, the hilt of the sword protruding behind its powerful shoulder. Fors rocked back and forth, his face twisted with pain, his fingers trying to rip away the cloth about a nasty-looking, freely bleeding slash down the outer side of his left leg above the knee.

Lura emerged from the bushes. There were unpleasant stains on her usually fastidiously kept coat and she moved with an air of general satisfaction. As she passed the boar she snarled and gave the body a raking clout with one front paw.

Fors worked his heel free from the rotten board which had clamped it and crawled toward the Star pouch. He needed water now—but Lura would sniff that out for him. The worst would be going lame for a while. He would be lucky if he did not have to stay where he was for a day or two.

Lura did find water, a spring a little beyond the farm-house. And he crawled to it painfully. With dry twigs he kindled a fire and set a tiny pan of the clear water to boil. Now he was ready for the worst—boar's tusks were notoriously dirty and deadly.

Setting his teeth he cut and tore away the cloth of his leggings until the skin around the still oozing slash was bare. Into the bubbling water he dropped a minute portion of the wound salve from the Star pouch. The secret of that slave belonged to the Healer of the tribe and the Captain of the Star Men alone. It was wisdom from the old days which had saved many lives. A wound anointed with it did not rot.

Fors let the water cool until he could just bear it and then poured more than half of it into that ragged tear in skin and muscle. His fingers were shaking when he thrust them into the water left in the pan, holding them there for a minute before tearing open the packet of bandage. With an end of the soft material he washed and dabbed delicately along the cut. Then he smeared some of the unheated paste across it and bound a pad tightly over it. The bleeding had almost stopped, but the wound was like a band of stinging fire from hip socket to ankle bone, and his eyes were misty as he worked, following the instructions which had been drilled into him since his first hunting trip.

At last he could put out the fire and lie quietly. Lura stretched out beside him and put a velvet-gloved paw on his arm. She purred soothingly, once or twice drawing her rough tongue across his flesh in her favorite caress. The burning in his leg eased, or else he was growing accustomed to the torment. He stared into the sky. Pink and gold streamed across it in wide swaths. It must be close to sundown. He would have to have shelter. But it was a struggle to move and his leg had stiffened so that even when he got up and clutched at bushes to pull himself along he made slow progress.

Lura went down the slope and he stumbled after her, glad that only tall grass covered most of it. She headed for the farmyard, but he did not call her back. Lura was hunting shelter for them both and she would find it, if any such existed.

She did bring him to the best housing they had had since they had left the Eyrie, a stone-walled, single-roomed building. He had no idea for what purpose it had been built. But there was only one door, no windows, and part of the roof was still in place. It could be easily defended and it was shelter.

Already small scavengers were busy about the bodies of the pigs. And with the dark the scent of blood would draw more formidable flesh eaters. He had not forgotten the quarrels over the bodies of the cow and calf. So Fors pushed loose stones into a barrier about his door and decided upon a fire. The walls would hide it from all but birds flying overhead.

He ate sparingly of dried corn. Lura jumped the barrier and went hunting on her own, questing through the twilight. But Fors nursed his point of fire and stared out into the gathering darkness. Fireflies made dancing sparks under the straggling limbs of ancient orchard trees. He watched them as he drank from the water in his canteen.

The pain in his leg was now a steady throb which arose into his head and settled in his temples—beat—beat—beat—

Then Fors suddenly realized that that steady rhythm was not born of pain and fever. There was an actual sound, hanging on the night air, low, carrying well, a measured note which bore no resemblance to any natural noise he had heard before. Only, something in it suggested the queer crooning song of the fisherman. If something not unlike the same series of notes was being tapped out on the head of a drum now—

Fors jerked upright. Bow and sword were within reach of his hand. The night, which was never as dark for him as it was for others, was peaceful and empty—save for that distant signal. Then it stopped, abruptly, almost in mid-note, with a suggestion of finality. He guessed that he would not hear it again. But what could it mean?

Sound carried well in these lowlands—even if listeners did not have his keenness of ear. A message sent by such a drum might carry safely across miles.

His fingernails dug into the flesh of his palms. There was a trace of sound again—coming from the far south—a disturbance in the air so faint it might only be born of his imagination.

But he did not believe that. The drummer was receiving an answer. Under his breath Fors counted off seconds—five, ten, fifteen, and then again silence. He tried to sort out his impressions of the fisherman—and again came to the same conclusion. He was not native to these lowlands, which meant that he was probably a scout, an explorer from the south. Who or what was now moving up into these lands?

4

Four Legs Are Better Than Two

EVEN BEFORE DAWN IT BEGAN to rain, a steady, straight downpour which would last for hours. Fors' wound was stiff and he had trouble crawling back into the corner of the hut where the broken roof still afforded some protection. Lura rolled against him and the warmth of her furry body was a comfort. But Fors was unable to drop back into the restless, dream-broken sleep which had held him most of the night.

It was the thought of the day's travel still before him which plagued him. To walk far would reopen the gash and he thought that he had a degree or so of fever. Yet he had to have food and better shelter. And that drumming— Being disabled he wanted to get out of the near vicinity of the drummer—fast.

As soon as it was light enough for him to distinguish a black line on white paper he got out his scrap of map, trying to guess his present position—if it were on that fragment at all. There were tiny red figures printed between certain points—the measured miles of the Old Ones who kept to the roads. By his reckoning he might

yet be at least three days' journey from the city—if, of
course, he was now where he believed himself to be.
Three days' journey for a strong and tireless traveler, not
for a crippled limper. If he had a horse now—

But the memory of Jarl with the horse herders put that
thought out of his mind. If he went to the Plains camp
and tried to trade, the Star Captain would hear of it. And
for a novice to steal a mount out of one of the well-
guarded herds was almost impossible even if he were
able-bodied. But he could not banish his wish—even by
repeating this argument of stern commonsense.

Lura went out hunting. She would bring back her kill.
Fors pulled himself up, clenching his teeth against the
pain that such movement gave his whole left side. He had
to have some sort of crutch or cane if he wanted to keep
going. There was part of a sapling among the wood within
reach. It appeared almost straight and he hacked it down
with his knife and trimmed off the branches. With this aid
he could get around, and the more he moved the more
the stiffness seemed to loosen. When Lura returned, a
plump bronze-feathered turkey dragging out of her jaws,
he was in a better frame of mind and ready to eat break-
fast.

But the pace at which they started out was not a
speedy one. Fors hissed between set teeth when now and
again his weight shifted too heavily on the left leg. He
turned instinctively into what once had been the lane
tying the farmstead to the road, and brushed between the
encroaching bushes, leaning heavily on his cane.

Rain made sticky mud of every patch of open ground
and he was afraid of slipping and falling. Lura kept up a
steady low whine of complaint against the weather and
the slowness of their travel. But she did not go off on her
own as she might have done had he been himself. And
Fors talked to her constantly.

The lane came to the road and he turned into that
since it went in the direction he wished. Soil had drifted

across the concrete and made mud patches which gave root to spiked plants; but, even with that, it was better footing for an almost one-legged man than the wet ground. Lura scouted ahead, weaving in and out of the bushes and tall grass along the side of the old thoroughfare, testing the wind for alien scents, now and then shaking head or paws vigorously to rid them of clinging raindrops.

All at once she bounded out of the brush to Fors, pushing against him with her body, forcing him gently back toward the ditch which ran nearby. He caught the urgency of her warning and scrambled to cover with all the speed he could muster. As he lay against the greasy red clay bank with his palms spread flat, he felt the pounding long before he heard the hoofs which caused it. Then the herd came into sight, trotting at an easy pace down the old road. For a moment or two Fors searched for the herders and then he realized that none of the horses wore the patches of bright paint which distinguished ownership among the Plainsmen. They must be wild. There were several mares with foals, a snorting stallion bearing the scars of battle on his shoulders, and some yearlings running free.

But there was one mare who had no foal. Her rough, ungroomed coat was a very dark red, her burr-matted tail and mane black. Now and again she dropped to the back, stopping to snatch a mouthful of herbage, a trick which at last earned her a sharp nip from the stallion. She squealed, lashed out with ready hoofs, and then ran swiftly, breaking ahead of the rest of the band. Fors watched her go with regret. If he had had his two feet under him she might have been a possible capture. But no use thinking of that.

Then the herd rounded a curve and was out of sight. Fors took a moment's breather before he pulled himself back on the road. Lura was there before him, kneading her front paws on a mat of grass, staring after the van-

ished horses. To her mind there was no difference between one of those foals and the calf she had pulled
down. Both were meat and so to be eaten. It was in her
mind to trail along behind such a wealth of food. Fors did
not argue with her. He still thought of the mare who ran
free and followed her own will.

They came up again with the herd before the hour was
past. The road made a sudden dip into a valley which was
almost cup-shaped. At the bottom rich grass grew tall and
there the herd grazed, the watching stallion standing
guard halfway up the rise.

But what caught Fors' eyes was the shell of a building
which stood almost directly below. Fire had eaten out its
interior so that only the crumbling brick of the outer walls
remained. He studied it carefully and then tried to identify
the horses beyond.

The mare was apart from the herd, grazing close to the
building. Fors wet his lips with his tongue tip. There was
just a chance—a very wild chance—

It would depend largely upon Lura's co-operation. And
that had never failed him yet. He turned to the great cat
and tried to form a mind picture of what must be done.
Slowly he thought out each point. Twice he went through
it and then Lura crouched and withdrew into the grass.

Fors wiped sweat and rain from his forehead and
started crawling in turn, edging down into a maze of
fallen bricks. They could never do it if the wind was not
just right. But fortune was favoring to that extent. He
swung himself up on a ledge above the widest gap in the
broken wall and unwound from his waist the light tough
cord all mountain men carried. The weighted noose at the
end was in his hand. Good, the rain had not affected it.
Now—!

He whistled, the clear call of one of the Eyrie country
birds. And he knew, rather than saw, that Lura was in
position and ready to move. If the wind would only
hold—!

Suddenly the mare tossed up her head, snorted, and stared suspiciously at a clump of bushes. At the same time the stallion reared and thundered forth a fierce challenge. But he was almost the full length of the valley away, and he stopped to send the rest of his harem out of danger before he came to the mare. She wanted to follow but plainly the hidden menace now lay between her and freedom. She whirled on two feet and pounded back in the direction of the ruin where Fors waited. Twice she tried to go with her mates and both times she was sent back on the opposite course.

Fors coiled his rope. He had only to wait and trust to Lura's skill. But the seconds that he was forced to do that were very long. At last the mare, her eyes white-rimmed with terror, burst through the gap in the masonry. Fors cast and as quickly snubbed the rope about a girder of rusting steel protruding from the brickwork. The heart of the metal was still sound enough to hold, even against the frantic plunges of the terrified horse. The scream of the aroused stallion, thundering down to the rescue, shook Fors. He did not know much about horses but he could imagine that there was danger now.

But the stallion never reached the ruin. Out of the bushes, directly at his head, leaped Lura, leaped and raked with cruel claws. The stallion reared, trumpeting like a mad thing, slashing out with teeth and hoofs. But Lura was only a flash of light fur covering steel springs and she was never there when the stallion struck. Twice more she got home with a wicked, slashing paw, before the horse gave up the battle and fled back down the valley, following the herd. The mare cried after him. He turned, but Lura was there, and her snarled warning sent him on again dripping blood.

Fors leaned back weakly against a pile of rubble. He had the mare all right, a rope about her neck, a rope which would hold her in spite of all her plunges and kicks. But here was no gentled mount already broken to ride.

And how was he, with a bad leg, to conquer the fear-maddened animal?

He made the rope fast, looking ruefully at the burns on his hands. Just now he could not get near her. Might be well to let her become used to captivity for an hour or so—to try to win her— But would she ever lose her fear of Lura? That was another problem to be solved. Only—it must be done, he could not go on in this one-legged way, and he certainly was not going to beg shelter from the Plains camp and so fall into Jarl's hands. He believed that he could make his own way in the lowlands—now was the time to prove that!

After a time the mare ceased to fight for freedom and stood with drooping head, nervous shudders running along her sweat-encrusted limbs and flanks. Fors stayed where he was but now he began to talk to her, using the same crooning tone with which he called Lura. Then he ventured to limp a few steps closer. Her head went up and she snorted. But he continued to talk to her, making an even monotone of his voice. At last he was close enough to touch her rough coat and as he did so he almost jumped. Still faintly sketched on the hide was a dab or two of fading paint! Then this was a Plainsman's mount from one of the tame herds. Fors gulped weakly. Such luck was a little uncanny. Now, seeing that, he dared to stroke her nose. She shivered under his touch and then she whinnied almost inquiringly. He patted her shoulder and then she nudged him playfully with her nose. Fors laughed, tugging at the ragged forelock which bobbed between her eyes.

"So now you remember, old lady? Good girl, good girl!"

There remained the problem of Lura and that must be solved as quickly as possible. He unfastened the rope and pulled gently. The mare came after him willingly enough, picking her way daintily through the piles of fallen brick.

Why hadn't she scented the cat on his clothes? Unless

the rain had dampened it— But she had shown no fright at his handling.

He whistled the bird call for the second time, after he had snubbed the mare's lead rope around a small tree. The answer to his summons came from down valley. Apparently Lura was following the herd. Fors stood talking to his captive as he waited. At last he ventured to rub down her flanks with tufts of grass. Then he felt her start and tremble and he turned.

Lura sat in the open, her tail curled neatly over her forepaws. She yawned, her red tongue pointing up and out, her eyes slitted, as if she had very little interest in the mare which her hunting companion chose to fondle so stupidly.

The mare jerked back to the full length of the rope, her eyes showing white. Lura took no notice of the open terror. At length she arose and stretched, then padded to the horse. The mare reared and gave a shrill scream. Fors tried to urge Lura back. But the big cat paced in a circle about the captive, eyeing her speculatively from all angles. The mare dropped back on four feet and shook her head, turning to keep her attention ever upon the cat. It seemed as if she were now puzzled when the attack she had expected had not come.

Maybe some message passed between the animals then. Fors never knew. But when Lura finished her inspection, she turned indifferently and the mare stopped trembling. However, it was more than an hour before Fors improvised a bridle from the rope and a saddle pad from his blanket. He climbed upon the bricks and managed to throw his good leg over the mare's back.

She had been well trained by the Plainsman who had owned her and her pace was so even that Fors, awkward and inexperienced at riding as he was, could keep his seat. He headed her back on the road which had brought him to the valley and they came up into the rolling fields once more.

In spite of the nagging ache of his wound Fors knew a surge of exultation and happiness. He had won safely out of the Eyrie, having plundered the Star House, he dared the lowlands, had spent one night in the heart of a dead town, had crossed a river through his own skill, spied successfully at the woods lake, faced the savage boar from which even the best of the mountain hunters sometimes fled, and now he had a horse under him, his weapons to hand, and the road open before him.

Judged unfit for the Star, cast aside by the Council was he? His even teeth gleamed in a grin which bore some likeness to Lura's hunting snarl. Well, they would see— see that Langdon's son, White Hair the Mutant—was as good as their best! He would prove that to the whole Eyrie.

Lura drifted back and the mare side-stepped as if she were still none too pleased to have the big cat venture so close. Fors jolted out of his daydreams, paid heed to his surroundings.

There were piles of rubble scattered through the brush, skeletons of old buildings, and, all at once, the mare's unshod hoofs raised a different sort of noise. She was picking her way across pavements in which were set long straight lines of rusted tracks. Fors pulled her up. Ahead the ruins were closer together and grew larger. A town—maybe even a small city.

There was something about these ruins which made him uneasy. The farms which had been recaptured by wild vegetation had none of this eerie strangeness about them. He knew again the faint sickness, neither of body nor spirit, which had gripped him on the road when he had traveled beside the wrecked convoy. Now he wiped one hand through the mare's coarse mane as if he would like to rub away an unpleasant smear. And yet he had touched nothing in this place. There was an evil miasma which arose mistlike even through the steady drizzle of rain.

Mist—there was real mist, too! Ahead he saw coils of dirty white drifting in, wreathing the tangled bulk of rotting wood and tumbled brick and stone. A fog was gathering, thicker than the mountain ones he had known, thick and somehow frightening. His fingers left the horse hair and flipped against his sore leg. The stab of pain which followed made him bite out a hot exclamation. This fog would put an end to travel for the day as far as he was concerned. Now he needed a safe place to hole up in where he could light a fire and prepare another treatment for his wound. And he wanted to be out of the rain for the night.

He did not like the ruins, but now they might hold what he needed and it was wiser to penetrate farther into them. But he held the mare to a slow walk and it was well that he did. For soon a break in the pavement opened before them—a gaping black hole rimmed with jagged teeth of broken concrete. They made a detour, edging as far from the crumbling lip as the ruins would allow. Fors began to regret leaving the stone hut on the farm. His constant pain he could no longer ignore. Perhaps it would have been better to have rested for a day or two back there. But if he had done that he would not now be riding the mare! He whistled softly and watched her ears point up in answer. No, it was worth even the grinding in his flesh to have such a mount.

Twice more the pavement was broken by great holes, the last being so large that it had the dimensions of a small crater. As Fors rode slowly around it he crossed a strip of muddy, but hard-beaten earth which came up out of its shadowed maw. It had the appearance of a well-worn and much-used path. Lura sniffed at it and snarled, her back fur roughened, and she spat with a violent hissing sound. Whatever made that path she counted an enemy.

Any creature which Lura, who would tackle a wild cow, a herd of roving swine, or a stallion, so designated was not one which Fors cared to meet in his present crippled state. He loosened rein and urged the mare to a brisker pace.

Some distance beyond the crater they came to a small hill on which stood a building of white stone, and it still possessed a roof. The slope of the hill was clear of all save a few low bushes and from the building Fors guessed one could have an almost unhampered view of the surrounding territory. He decided quickly in its favor.

It was a disappointment to discover that the roof covered only a part and that the center was open to the storm—being a small amphitheater in which rows of wide seats went down to a square platform.

However, there were small rooms around the outer rim, under the roof, and in one of these he made camp. He tied the mare to one of the pillars forming the aisle to the amphitheater and contented her with grass pulled from the hill and some of his parched corn which she relished. She could have been hobbled and left to graze but the memory of that worn path by the crater kept him from doing that.

Rain had collected in broken squares of the pavement and Lura drank eagerly from one such pool while the mare sucked noisily at another. From the drift of wind-driven branches caught among the pillars Fors built a fire, placed behind a wall so that it could not be observed from below. Water boiled in his pan and he went through the ordeal of redressing the gash in his leg. The salve was working, for the flesh was sore and stiff but it was clean and without infection, and the edges were already closing, though undoubtedly he would be scarred for the rest of his life.

Lura made no move to go hunting, although she must have been hungry. In fact, since she had skirted the crater she had kept close to him, and now she lay beside the fire, staring into the flames broodingly. He did not urge her to go out. Lura was more woodswise than any man could hope to be and if she did not choose to hunt there was good reason for her decision. Fors only wished that she could reveal to him the exact nature of the thing she both hated and feared. That hatred and fear came through to him when their minds held fleeting touch, but the creature which aroused such emotions remained a secret.

So they went hungry to bed since Fors determined to use what was left of his corn to bind the mare to him. He kept the fire burning low for he did not want to lie in the dark here where there were things beyond his knowledge.

For a time he listened for the drumming of the night before. He fully expected to hear it again. But the night was still. It had stopped raining at last, and he could hear insects in the grass outside. There was the murmur of a breeze through the foliage on the hill.

It made Fors uneasy, that faint sad soughing. Lura was not asleep either. He sensed her restlessness even before he heard the pad of her paws and saw her move toward the door. He crawled after her, trying to spare his leg. She had halted at the outer portico of the building and was looking down into the blackness of the ruined city. Then he saw what held her—a pin point of red to the north— the telltale flicker of fire flame!

So there was other life here! Plainsmen for the most part kept clear of the ruins—in memory of the old days when radiation killed. And the Beast Things—did they possess the secret of fire? No man knew how much or how little they had in the way of intelligence or perverted civilization.

The urge to get the mare, to crawl up on her back and cross the rubble to that distant fire, was strong. Fire and companionship in this place of the restless dead—they pulled at Fors now.

But before he so much as filled his lungs again he heard it—a low chorus of yapping, barking, howling which rose higher and higher to a frenzied bedlam. Lura's hair was stiff under his hand. She hissed and snarled, but she did not stir. The cries were coming from some distance—from the direction of the fire. Whatever manner of beast made them had been drawn by that.

Fors shuddered. There was nothing he could do to aid the fire maker. Long before he could find his slow way through the ruins the end would have come. And now—now—there was only blackness down there! The flicker of friendly red was gone!

5

⬙   The City on the Lake

FORS DRAGGED HIMSELF OUT INTO the morning sun. He
had slept poorly, but he was content that his wound was
healing. And, after he once got to his feet, he managed
better, being able without too much effort to take the
mare out to graze on the hillside. Lura had been on duty
before he roused, as the body of a plump turkey laid on
the floor by the remains of the fire testified. He broiled it
and ate, knowing all the time that when he was done he
must mount and ride across the shattered town searching
out the site of that fire which had vanished in the night.

And he did not want to take that ride. Because he did
not want to, he finished quickly, gathering up his supplies
with nervous haste. Lura came back and sat in the broad
beam of sunlight washing her fur. But she was on her feet
instantly as Fors got up on the mare and turned into the
heart of the ruins.

They clattered out into a burned area where the black
stain of a vast, devouring fire had not faded. There were
flowers growing there among the sooty stones, yellow,
white, and blue. And a ragged, red-leafed weed overran

55

old cellars. Cat and horse moved slowly through the desolation, testing their footing.

On the far edge of the burned space they found the scene of that night battle. Black birds whirred up from almost under their feet, birds which had been feasting on scraps more powerful scavengers had left them. Fors dismounted and limped up to the trampled grass, reluctant to make investigation.

Two well-picked piles of bones lay on the bloodstained ground. But the skulls were not those of his own race. Those long narrow heads with the cruel yellow teeth he had never seen before. Then the glint of metal caught his eyes and he picked up a broken spear, the haft snapped raggedly off not far from the head. And that spear he *had* seen before! It belonged to the fisherman of the islet.

Fors moved around the circle of the battlefield. He came across one more of the strange skeletons, but, save for the spear, there was no other trace of the hunter. Lura exhibited a violent distaste for the bones—as if the odd scent which clung to them was utterly offensive. And now she stood on her hind legs and sniffed inquiringly up the side of a heap of bricks and stone.

So that was what had happened! The hunter had not been overwhelmed by a rush out of the dark. He had had time to clamber up where the night-running things could not attack in force, had been able from above to fight them off and leave the wounded and dead to the tearing teeth of their own companions. And he must have escaped—since *his* bones were not in evidence.

Fors kicked through the underbrush a last time just to be sure. Something round and brown rolled away from his toe. He reached for a small, well-polished drum fashioned of dark wood, the stretched head of hide cured to an almost metallic smoothness. The signal drum! Impulsively he tapped the head, and started at the low throbbing note which echoed through the ruins.

When he rode on the drum went with him. Why he did

not know, except that he was fascinated by such a message-sending device unknown to his own people.

Within a half hour the ruins lay behind. Fors was glad to be out in the clean freedom of the country again. All morning he rode at a leisurely pace, watching for any signs which the hunter might leave. He was sure that the man was striking north with almost as definite a purpose as the one which drew him in that direction. And, with the drum gone, there would be no more signals.

The next two days were quiet. There was no indication that the Plainsmen had ever ventured into this territory and the land was a hunters' paradise teeming with game. Fors wasted none of his precious arrows but left the chase to Lura who enjoyed every moment of it. And he varied his diet with berries and the ripe grain which grew wild in the ancient fields.

They avoided two more small towns, cutting around when they saw the first ruins. The dank, moldy places had little appeal and Fors had once or twice speculated as to what might have happened that night had he been the one caught in the open by the hunting pack, too crippled to climb to the safety the unknown had found. Now his leg was less painful, he walked a part of each day, stretching the muscles and toughening tender flesh. Most of the ache was gone and soon he would be able to move as freely as ever.

On the morning of the fourth day they came out upon a waste of sand- and wind-carved dunes and saw the great lake of legend. There was no end to the gray-blue expanse of water—it must be almost as large as the distant sea. High piles of bleached driftwood lay along the shore. There must have been a recent storm for the bodies of fish lay there too. Fors' nose wrinkled as he plowed through the sand, the mare sinking deeply as she followed him. Lura, investigating the fish, strayed some yards behind.

So—this much was true—this was the lake. And somewhere along its shore must lie the city his father had sought. Right or left, east or west—that was the question. He found shelter from the wind behind a dune and squatted down to consult the scrap of map. When they had avoided that last town they had gone west—so now—east. He would keep to the shore and see—

It was hard to travel in the sand, and after some time he gave up in disgust and edged inland to the more solid earth. Within two yards he was on a road! And, since the roadway hugged the shoreline, he held to it. Shortly the familiar mounds of debris closed in. But this was the remains of no small town. Even in his inexperience he could judge that. In the morning sun far ahead he saw battered towers rising in the sky. This was one of the cities, the great cities of huge sky-reaching towers! And it was not a "blue" one either. He would have seen the sign of that taint on the sky in the night.

His city—all his! Langdon had been right—this was an untouched storehouse waiting to be looted for the benefit of the Eyrie. Fors allowed the mare to amble on at her own pace as he tried to recall all the training rules. Libraries—those were what one was to look for—and shops, especially those which had stores of hardware or paper or kindred supplies. One was not to touch food— no matter if it was found in unbroken containers. Experimentation of that kind had brought death by poisoning too many times in the past. Hospital supplies were best of all, but those had to be selected by the trained expert. Danger lay too in unknown drugs.

For his looting he had best take only samples of what was to be found—books, writing supplies, maps, anything which would prove that he knew how to select intelligently. And with the mare he ought to be able to pack out quite a lot.

Here were signs of fire, too. He rode across a bare stretch where the rough footing was all black ash. But the towers stood taller and they did not appear to be too badly damaged. If this city had been bombed, would they be standing at all? Maybe this was one of the places which had perished in the plagues which followed the war. Maybe it had died slowly with the ebbing life of its people—and not suddenly in explosion.

The road they had been following was now a narrow gorge between tall ranks of broken buildings, the upper stories of which had fallen into the street in mounds which almost blocked it completely at places. Here were numerous surface machines in which the Old Ones had ridden in comfort. And here, also, were bones. That single skull he had found in the old bank had had the power to shake him a little, but here lay a nation of dead and soon he ceased to notice them at all, even when the mare trod on brittle ribs or kicked rolling skulls aside. Yes, now it was very apparent that the men of this city had died of plague, or gas, or even of the radiation sickness. But sun and wind and animals had cleared away the foulness of that death, leaving only a framework without power to harm.

As yet Fors did not attempt to explore those caverns which had once been the lower floors of the buildings. Now he only wanted to get on into the very heart of the place, to the foundations of those towers which had guided him all morning. But before he could reach that goal a barrier was laid across his road.

There was a gash breaking the city in two, a deep valley which nursed a twisted river in its middle. Bridges spanned it. He came to the lip of one such span and he could see two others. But before him was a mass of rusting wreckage piled into a fantastic wall. Machines—not in ones and twos or even in tens, but in hundreds—were packed as they must have crashed and telescoped into one another, driven by men who feared some danger behind enough to drive in crazy flight. The bridge was now one gigantic crack-up. Fors might be able to scramble across but the mare could not. It would be best to descend into the valley and cross there—because as far as he could see the other bridges were also choked with rust-eaten metal.

There was a side road down into the valley, and machines filled it too. Men had taken that same trail when the bridge jammed. But the three of them—horse, cat and man—worked their way through to reach the river level. Tracks were rust-red lines and on them were trains—the first he had ever seen. Two had crashed together, the engine of one plowing into the other. Those who had tried to escape by train had been little better off than their brothers in the stalled cars above. It was difficult for Fors to imagine what that last wild day of flight must have been—the trains, the machines. He knew of them only from the old books. But the youngsters of the Eyrie sometimes stirred up nests of black ants and watched them boil up and out. So this city must have boiled—but few had been able to win out.

And those who had—what became of them in the end? What could help a handful of panic-stricken refugees scattered over a countryside, perhaps dropping dead of the plague as they fled? Fors shivered as he picked his way along beside the wrecked trains. But when he found a narrow path through the jumble he was in luck. There had been barges on the river and they had drifted and sunk to form a shaky bridge across the water. Horse, man, and cat started over it, testing each step. There was a gap in the middle through which the stream still fought its way. But the mare, under the urging of Fors' heels in her ribs, jumped it and Lura went sailing over with her usual agility.

More dark streets with blank-eyed buildings lining them, and then there was a road leading up at a sharp angle. They took it to find themselves at last close to the towers. Birds wheeled overhead, crying out in thin sharp voices, and Fors caught a glimpse of a brownish animal slithering out of sight through a broken doorway. Then he came up to a wall which was part glass, miraculously unbroken, but so besmeared by the dust and wind-driven grime of the years that he could not see what lay behind it. He dismounted and went over, rubbing his hands across that strange smoothness. The secret of fashioning such perfect glass was gone—with so many other secrets of the Old Ones.

What he saw beyond his peephole nearly made him retreat, until he remembered the Star Men's tales. Those were not the Old Ones standing within the shadowed cavern, but effigies of themselves which they put up in shops to show off clothing. He pasted his nose to the glass and stared his fill at the three tall women and the draperies of rotting fabric still wreathed about them. None of that would, he knew, survive his touch.

It always turned to dust in the grasp of any explorer who tried to handle it.

There were other deep show windows about him but all had been denuded of their glass and were empty. Through them one could get into the stores behind. But Fors was not yet ready to go hunting, and probably there would be little there now worth carrying away.

The building to his left was topped with a tall tower which reached higher into the heavens than any other around it. From the top of that a man might see the whole city, to measure its size and environs. But he knew that the Old Ones had movable cars rising in such buildings, the power for which was dead. There might not be any steps—and if there were his lame leg was not yet ready for climbing. Maybe before he left the city— It would be a workmanlike project to make a sketch of the city as seen from that tower—an excellent embellishment to a formal report.

That was the nearest he came to admitting even to himself that he had hopes of a future within the Eyrie, that he dreamed of standing before the elders of the Council and proving that he, the rejected mutant, had accomplished what others had been trained for all their lives long. When he thought of that he was warm deep inside. A new city—the one his father had sought—all mapped and explored, ready for the systematic looting of the Eyrie—what could a man who reported that ask for as a reward? Just about what he wanted—

Fors went on slowly, afoot now, with the mare trailing him and Lura scouting ahead. Neither animal appeared to want to stray too far. The sound of a rolling stone, the cries of the birds, all echoed through the empty buildings eerily. For the first time Fors wished for a companion of his own breed—in a place where only the dead had lain so long it would be good to call upon the living.

The sun was overhead and it was reflected from a shelf in the forepart of a shop. Fors swung over a strip of iron embedded in concrete to investigate. Rings lay there, rows of them, set with brilliant white stones—diamonds he guessed. He sorted them out of the dust and litter. Most of them were too small to fit any of his fingers, but he chose four of the largest stones to take along—with some vague idea of surprising the young of the Eyrie. Among them was one broader band with a deep red gem and this slipped on to his third finger as if it had been fashioned for it. He turned it around, pleased with the deep crimson shade of the stone. It was a good omen, discovering it, as if the long dead craftsmen had made it for him. He would wear it for luck.

But food would be more useful than sparkling stones now. The mare must eat and they would not find grazing hereabouts. In this section there was only a wild waste of ruins. He must head out toward the edge of the city if he wanted a real camping place. Not through the valley of the trains, though. It would be better to measure the extent of the city by trying to get through it to the opposite side—if he could do that by nightfall.

Fors did not stop to explore any more of the shops, but he made mental notes about those which might be worth a second visit. It was slow work breaking a trail through the blocked streets, and the heat reflected back from the buildings brought sweat dripping from his face to plaster his clothing to him. He had to mount again as his leg began to ache, and the hollow feeling in his middle grew worse. Lura protested—she wanted to get away from this wilderness of stone, into the fields where one could hunt.

Three hours of steady traveling brought them through to the edge of the enchanted wood, for that was what it seemed. It was a band of living green cutting across the pitiless heat and barrenness of the ruins. Once it had been a park, but now it arose a true forest which Lura welcomed with an open meow of delight. The mare whinnied, bursting through bushes until she came into what was undoubtedly a game trail leading down a gentle slope. Fors dismounted and let the mare go on, her pace now a trot. They reached the end of the trail, a lake. The mare stood, nose- and hock-deep, in the green water. Long red-gold fish swam away from the disturbance she caused.

Fors dropped down on a wide stone and pulled off his boots to dabble his burning feet in the coolness. There was a breeze across the water which dried his damp body and lifted the leaves of the wild shrubs around them. He looked across the lake. Opposite him there was a flight of broad white steps, cracked and moss-grown, and he caught a glimpse of a building at their head. But that could be explored later. Just now it was good to sit in the cool. The mare came out of the lake and tore up mouthfuls of the long grass. A duck quacked and fled from under her hoofs, sailing out on the water, swimming energetically toward the steps.

The evening was long, the twilight soft about the hidden lake. While there was still light enough to see Fors ventured into the tall, pillared building at the head of the stairs and discovered that his luck was still holding. It was a museum—one of those treasure houses which rated very high on the Star Men's list of desirable finds. He wandered through the high-ceiled rooms, his boots making splotchy tracks in the fine dust crisscrossed with the spoor of small animals. He brushed the dust from the tops of cases and tried to spell out the blotched and faded signs. Grotesque stone heads leered or stared blindly through the murk, and tatters of powdery canvas hung dismally from worm-eaten frames in what had once been picture galleries.

But the dark drove him out to shelter in the forecourt. Tomorrow would be time to estimate the worth of what lay within. Tomorrow—why, he had limitless time before him to discover and assess all that this city held! He had not even begun to explore.

It was warm and he allowed his cooking fire to burn down to a handful of coals. The forest was coming to life. He identified the bark of a questing fox, the mournful call of night birds. In the city streets he could almost imagine the gathering of wistful, hungry ghosts seeking what was gone forever. But here, where man had never lived, it was very peaceful and like the glens of his own mountain land. His hand fell on the pouch of the Star Men. Had Langdon actually walked here before him, had it been on a return trip from this place that his father had been killed? Fors hoped that was true—that Langdon had known the joy of proving his theory right—that his map had led him here before his death.

Lura appeared out of the shadows, padding lightly up the mossy steps from the water's edge. And the mare moved in without urging, her hoofs ringing on the broken marble as she came to join them. It was almost—Fors straightened, regarded the gathering night more intently—almost as if they feared an alien world enough to seek company against it. And yet he did not feel the unease he had known in those other ruins—this slice of woodland held no terrors.

Nevertheless he roused and went to gather as much wood as he could find and he worked with mounting haste until it was too dark to see at all, ending with a pile of broken branches and storm drift which might have been gathered to withstand a siege. Lura watched him—and beyond him—sitting sentry-wise at the head of the stairs. Nor did the mare move again into the open.

At last, his hands shaking a little with fatigue, the odd drive still urging him to some sort of effort, Fors strung his bow and set it close to hand, loosened his sword in its sheath. The wind had gone down. It was almost sultry. Above the water the birds had ceased to wheel.

There was a sudden thunder clap and a flash of violet lightning crossed the southern sky. Heat lightning, but there might be another storm on the way. That was probably what made the air seem electric. But Fors did not deceive himself. Something besides a storm was brooding out in that night.

Back in the Eyrie—when they watched the wintertime singplays—just before they drew up the big screen and the play began, he had had a queer feeling like this. A sort of excited waiting—that was it. And something else was waiting now—holding its breath a little. He squirmed. His imagination—he was cursed with too much of that!

A little was good. Langdon had always said that imagination was a tool to be used and no Star Man was any good without it. But when a man had too much—then it fed the dark fears way down inside and there was always an extra foe to fight in any battle.

But now, thinking of Langdon had not banished his strange feeling. Something was outside, dark and formless, brooding, watching—watching a tiny Fors beside a spark of puny fire—watching for some action—

He poked the fire viciously. Getting as silly as a moon-mad woodsrunner! There must be a madness which lay in wait in these dead cities to trap a man's thoughts and poison him. A more subtle poison it was than any the Old Ones had distilled to fight their disastrous wars. He must break that grip on his mind—and do it quickly!

Lura watched him from across the fire, her blue eyes

fired with topaz by the flames. She purred hoarsely, reassuringly. Fors relaxed a fraction of his guard. Lura's mood was an antidote. From the pouch he brought out the route book and began to enter—with painstaking attention and his best script—observations on the day's journey. If it was ever to be laid before Jarl it must measure up to the standard of such reports. The dark made a black circle beyond the reaches of the firelight.

6

THE NEXT DAY GAVE THREAT of being sultry. Fors awakened beset with a dull headache and vague memories of unpleasant dreams. His leg pained him. But when he examined the healing wound it showed no signs of the infection he dreaded. He longed for a swim in the lake but dared not try it until the throbbing seam had totally closed, being forced to content himself with splashing in the shallows.

Inside the museum the air was dead and there was a faint taint of decay hanging in the long chill corridors. Sightless masks hung on the walls and when he tested some of the displayed swords and knives they broke in brittle fragments.

In the end he took very little—much of the exhibit was too delicate to transport or too large. He chose some tiny figurines from a case where the dusty card said something about "Egypt" and a clumsy finger ring set with a carving of a beetle from a neighboring shelf. Last of all was a small sleek black panther, smooth and cool to his fingers, which he fell in love with and could not bear to leave behind. He did not venture into the side wings—not with all the city waiting for him.

But the museum was safe. Here were no falling walls and the alcove where he had spent the night was excellent shelter. He piled up his supplies in one corner before he sallied forth.

The mare was reluctant to leave the woods and the lake, but Fors' steady pull on her lead rope brought her back to the edge of the ruins. They went at a slow pace as he wanted to see what lay behind the spear points of glass which still clung in the shattered frames of the windows. These had all once been shops. How much of the wares they displayed were still worth plundering he could not guess. But he turned away in disappointment from fabrics eaten by insects and rotted by time.

In the fourth shop he entered was something much better. An unbroken glass case contained a treasure even greater than all the museum had to offer. Shut out from dust and most of the destruction of time were boxes of paper—whole boxes with blocks of separate sheets—and also pencils!

Of course the paper was brittle, yellowed, and easily torn. But in the Eyrie it could be pulped and re-worked into serviceable sections. And the pencils! There were few good substitutes for those. And the third box he opened held colored ones! He sharpened two with his hunting knife and made glorious red and green lines on the dusty floor. All of these must go with him. In the back of the shop he found a metal box which still seemed sturdy enough and into it he crammed all that he could. This— from just one shop! What riches could be expected from the city!

Why, here the men of the Eyrie could explore and loot perhaps for years before they exhausted all the supplies to be found. The only safe cities they had discovered before had been known to other tribes and were combed almost clean—or else they had been held by the Beast Things and were unsafe.

Fors tramped on, bits of glass crunching under his boots, skirting piles of rubble he could not clamber over. Such piles barricaded some shops entirely or else the roofs were unsafe. He was several blocks beyond the shop of the paper before he came to a second easy to enter. It had been another dealing in rings and gems. But the interior was in wild disorder as if it had been looted before. Cases lay smashed and the glass mingled with metal and stones on the floor. He stood in the doorway—it would take a long time to sort through that litter and the effort was not necessary. Only—as he turned away—he caught sight of something else on the floor which brought him back.

There was a patch of mud, dried brick-hard. And pressed deep into its surface, holding the pattern as if in a cast, was part of a footprint. He had seen its like before, near the pool of fresh deer blood. Those long narrow toe marks with the talon nail indentations could never be forgotten. That other print had been fresh. This was old. It might have been made months, even years before. The mud which held it crumbled under the prod of his finger tip. Fors backed out of the shop and stood with his back to a tumbling wall. The instinctive reaction which had made him do that also sent his eyes up and down the street.

Birds nested in the broken windows of the building across from him, flitting in and out on their own concerns. And not ten feet away a large gray rat sat on a pile of brick combing its fur and watching him with almost intelligent interest. It was a very large rat and a singularly fearless one. But no rat had made that footprint.

Fors summoned Lura from her ranging. With the cat to scout for him he would feel safer against attack. But he was still conscious of the many places where death could lurk, behind walls, in the pits which broke the street, in the open store fronts.

In the next hour he went about a mile, keeping to the main street and visiting only those buildings which Lura declared safe. The mare carried an odd assortment of bundles and he realized that he could not hope to transport more than a few selected samples of the abundance. He must cache part of his morning's finds in the museum and take only the cream of his gleanings south. Now that the city was discovered the men from the Eyrie would "work" it with greater efficiency, sending experts to choose and dismantle what they needed most and could best use. So the sooner he started back with the news, the more time they would have to work here before the coming of the bad weather in the fall.

The day grew even warmer and big black flies came out of the crevices of the stones to bite viciously, making the mare so crazy he could hardly control her. He had best head back now to the green and the lake and there sort over his loot. But, as they passed the place where he had found the wealth of paper, he stepped in for a last check upon all he must leave behind. The sun made a bright bar across the floor bringing into prominence the pencil marks he had made there. But—he was certain he had not used a yellow or blue pencil, although there had been a few.

Now—yellow and blue lines crisscrossed the red and green ones he had left—almost challengingly. The boxes of pencils he had piled for later transportation had been opened and two were gone!

He could see the tracks in the floor dust—his own boot-heel pattern and across that a more shapeless outline. And in the corner by the door someone had spit out the stone of a cherry!

Fors whistled in Lura. She examined the evidence on the floor and waited for instructions. But she was displaying none of the disgust with which she had greeted that earlier spoor. This might have been left by a roving Plainsman who was exploring the city on his own. If that were so, it behooved Fors to move quickly. He must get back to the Eyrie and return with help before some other tribe staked out a fair claim to the riches here. Once or twice before the mountaineers had been so disappointed.

Now there would be no question about leaving most of the spoil he had gathered. He must cache it in the museum and travel as light as possible to make time. Frowning, he stamped out of the shop and jerked at the mare's lead rope.

They came into the woods, cutting across a glade in the general direction of the museum. The mare snorted as they passed the end of the lake. Fors tugged her along by main force, bringing her up the steps to be relieved of her load. He packed the bundles into the room he now considered his own and freed the mare for grazing. Lura would keep watch until he had time to get everything in order.

But when Fors spread out the morning's loot on the floor he found it very difficult to pick and choose. If he took this—then he could not carry that—and *that* might make a greater impression upon the experts of the Eyrie. He made piles, only to completely change their contents three and four times over. But in the end he made up a pack which he hoped would best display to the mountain clan the quality of this find and be a good example of his own powers of selection. The rest could be easily concealed somewhere in the rambling halls of this building until he returned.

He sighed as he began to sort the discards into order. There was so much to be left behind—why, he should have a pack train of horses, such as the Plains tribes used to carry their gear on the march. The drum rolled and he picked it up, rubbing his fingers across its top to hear again the queer pulsing sound. Then he tapped with his nails and the sound echoed weirdly through the halls.

This must have been the drum which had sounded through the night after his fight with the boar. A signal—! He could not resist other experimental thumps—and then tried out the rhythm of one of his own mountain hunting songs. But this strong music was more eerie than any from the flute or the three- and four-stringed harps his people knew.

As the frightening rumble died away Lura flowed in, her eyes uncannily aglow, haste and urgency expressed in every dark hair on her head. He must come with her and at once. Fors dropped the drum and reached for his bow. Lura stood by the door, her tail tip flicking.

She went down the steps in two bounds and he went after her, not sparing his leg. The mare was standing in the shallows of the lake undisturbed. Lura glided on, between trees and bushes and into the thick depths of the wood. Fors followed at a slower pace, not being able to move so quickly through the green obstruction.

But before he had gone out of sight of the lake he heard it—a faint moaning cry, almost a sigh, which had been wrung out of real suffering. It arose to a hoarse croak, framing muffled words he did not understand. But human lips had shaped them, he was sure of that. Lura would not have guided him to one of the Beast Things.

The gabble of strange words died away into another moan which seemed to rise out of the ground before him. Fors shied away from an expanse of dried grass and leaves which lay there. Lura had dropped to her belly, reaching out with a forepaw to feel delicately of the ground, not advancing into the small clearing.

One of the pits which he had found throughout the city was Fors' first thought—at any rate a hole of some sort. Now he could see a break through at the opposite end of this cleared space. He started to edge around, treading on the half-exposed roots of trees and bushes and holding on firmly to anything which looked sturdy.

From the torn gap in the mat of dried grass and brush

rose a sickening stench. Trying to spare his leg he went to his knees and peered into the dusk below. What he saw there set his stomach to churning.

It was a wicked trap—that pit—a trap artfully constructed and skillfully concealed with the matted covering. And it held its victims. The small deer had been dead for days, but the other body which, as his eyes adjusted to the dim light, he saw writhe weakly, must have lain there for a shorter time. The blood on the impaled shoulder still ran free.

Sharp-pointed stakes had been set in the earth at the bottom, pointing upward to catch and hold the fallen for a tortured death. And the man who half hung, half lay there now had escaped that death by less than six inches.

He had struggled to free himself, as the gaping wound in his own flesh testified, but all his strength had not brought him loose. Fors measured the space between the stakes and then looked around for a good-sized tree. This would not be easy—

It did not take long to fetch what was left of his climbing rope and make a noose in it. The man in the pit looked up with glazed eyes. Whether he could see or understand what his rescuer was planning Fors did not know. He fastened the end of the cord to an arrow and shot the line over the branch which hung the closest to the trap.

To make one end of the rope fast to the tree took only an instant. Then, with the other in his hand, Fors lowered himself cautiously over the edge of the pit, using his elbows to break his speed as he slipped down to the smeared stakes. Black flies rose in a noxious cloud and he had to beat them off as he reached the side of the prisoner. The belt about the fellow's middle was tight enough and he knotted the rope.

The way out of the pit was more difficult, since the makers had fashioned it with every precaution against that very operation. But a landslide at one end gave some

footing and Fors fought his way back to the top. It was
plain that whoever had set that pitfall had not visited it
for some time and Fors left the sentry duty to Lura.

This was going to be a nasty business, but it was the
only way he could see of saving the sufferer below. He un-
tied the rope end on the tree and twisted it about his
wrists. Lura came without being summoned and seized
the dangling tip in her jaws. Together they gave their
weight to a quick jerk which was answered by a wild
scream of agony. But Fors did not lessen the steady pull
and Lura matched him step by step as he crept back.

Out of the black hole rose the lolling head and bloody
shoulders of the stranger. When he swung clear Fors
made fast the rope and hurried back to pull the limp body
away from the edge of the fiendish mantrap. His hands
were slippery with blood before he got the unconscious
man free. He could not carry the fellow, not with his bad
leg. Also he must weigh more than Fors by forty pounds.
For, now that he lay in the sunlight, Fors recognized him
as the dark-skinned hunter of the island. But his big body
was flaccid and his face greenish white under its brown
pigment. At least the blood was not spurting from that
wound—no artery had been touched. He must get the
stranger back to the museum where he could see to the
ugly tear—

There was a crashing in the brush. Fors hurled himself
for the bow which lay where he had dropped it. But it
was Lura who came out, urging the mare before her. The
scent of blood made the mare roll her eyes and circle
away, but Fors wanted no nonsense now and Lura was of
a like mind. She walked up to the horse and gave several
low snarls. The mare stood still, sweating, her eyes
showing white. But she did not rear as Fors somehow got
his patient across her back.

Once back in the shelter of the museum he gave a sigh
of relief and rolled the stranger onto his blanket. The
other's eyes were open again and this time with the light

of reason in their dark brown depths. The hunter was very young. Now that he was so helpless this was plain. He could not count many more years than did Fors himself—in spite of his big frame and wide, well-muscled shoulders. He lay in quiet patience watching Fors make a fire and prepare the salve, but he said nothing, even when the mountaineer went to work with his crude surgery.

The stake had passed through the skin of the shoulder, tearing a wicked gouge, but, Fors saw with relief, breaking no bones. If infection did not develop the stranger would recover.

His handling of that torn flesh must have caused the stranger agony but he made no sound, although when Fors finished at last beads of bright crimson showed along the other's lower lip. He made a gesture with his good hand toward the pouch at his belt and Fors unfastened it. He selected with rumbling fingers a small bag of white material and pushed it into his rescuer's hand, jerking his thumb at the pannikin of water Fors had used during his surgery. There was a coarse brownish meal in the bag. Fors drew fresh water, shook in a little of the stuff and set it back on the fire. His patient nodded and smiled weakly. Then he stabbed himself in the chest with a forefinger and said:

"Arskane—"

"Fors," and then pointing to Lura the mountaineer added, "Lura."

Arskane nodded his head and added a sentence in a deep, almost rolling voice which had a drum note in it. Fors frowned. Some of those words—yes, they were like his own speech. The accent, though, was different—there was a slurring of certain sounds. He tried in his turn.

"I am Fors of the Puma Clan from the Smoking Mountains—" He tried gestures to piece out meaning.

But Arskane sighed. His face was drawn and tired and his eyes closed wearily. Plainly he could not make the effort for coherent speech now. Fors' chin rested on the palm of his hand and he stared into the fire. This was going to alter his own plans drastically. He could not go away and leave Arskane alone, unable to fend for himself. And the big man might not be able to travel for days. He would have to think about this.

The boiling water began to give off a fragrant odor—new to his nostrils but enticing. He sniffed the steam as the water turned brown. When the liquid was quite dark he took a chance and pulled the pan off to cool. Arskane stirred and turned his head. He smiled at the steam arising from the water and gestured that when it was ready he would drink.

This, then, must be the medicine of his own people. Fors waited, tested it with a cautious finger tip, and then raised the dark head on his arm, holding the pan to those bitten lips. Half the liquid was gone before Arskane signed he had enough. He motioned for Fors to try it too, but a single bitter mouthful was enough to satisfy the mountaineer. It tasted far worse than it smelled.

For the rest of the afternoon Fors was busy. He hunted with Lura, bringing back the best parts of a deer they surprised at the end of the lake, and some of the quail flushed out of the grass. He added an uncounted number of armloads to the stack of firewood. There were berries, too, won from a briary thicket. And, when at last he threw himself down beside the fire and stretched out his aching leg, he was so tired he thought that he could not move again. But now they were provisioned for more than one day ahead. The mare had shown a tendency to wander off, so he shut her into one of the long corridors for the night.

Arskane was awake again after the fitful feverish sleep of the afternoon, and he watched as Fors prepared the birds for broiling. He ate, but not as much as Fors offered. The mountaineer was worried. There might have been poison upon those trap stakes. And he had nothing with which to combat that. He heated up the bitter brown water and made Arskane drink it to the dregs. If there was any virtue in the stuff the big man needed all its help now.

As it grew dark Fors' patient fell asleep again but his attendant hunched close to the fire, even though the evening was warm. The mantrap was occupying his thoughts. True, all the evidence pointed to its not being visited for a long time by those who had set it. The trapped deer in it had been dead for days and there had been another skeleton, picked clean by insects and birds, at the other end of the hole. But someone or something had spent much labor and time in its construction, and it had been devised by a mind both cunning and cruel. No Plainsman he had ever heard of followed that crafty method of hunting, and it was certainly not to the taste of the men of the Eyrie. It was new to Arskane, or he would not have fallen a victim to it. So that meant others—not of the plains or of the mountains or of Arskane's tribe—others roaming this city at their will. And in the cities there lived at ease only—the Beast Things!

Fors' mouth was dry, he rubbed his hands across his knees. Langdon had died under the throwing darts and the knives of the Beast Things. Others of the Star Men had met them—and had not returned from that meeting. Jarl wore a crooked red seam down his forearm which was the result of a brush with one of their scouts. They were horrible, monstrous—not human. Fors was mutant—yes. But he was still human. These were not. And it was because of the Beast Things that mutants were so feared. For the first time he began to understand that. There was a purpose behind the hatred of the mutants. But he was human! And the Beast Things were not!

He had never seen one, and the Star Men who had and survived never talked about them to the commoners of the Eyrie. Legend made them boogies of the dark— ogres—foul things of the night.

What if it had been a Beast Thing trap Arskane had

been caught in? Then the Things must live here. There were thousands upon thousands of hiding places in the ruins to shelter them. And only Lura's instinct and hunting skill, and his own ears and eyes to guard them. He looked out into the dusk and shivered. Ears and eyes, bow and sword, claws and teeth—maybe none of those would be enough!

7

Death Plays Hide and Seek

FOR FOUR DAYS ARSKANE LAY in the cool hall of the museum while Fors hunted for the pot or ranged in scouting trips through the woodland, never venturing too far from the white building. And at night across the fire they grew familiar with each other's speech and exchanged stories of their past.

"Our Old Ones were flying men," Arskane's deep voice rolled across the room. "After the Last Battle they came down from the sky to their homeland and found it blasted into nothing. Then they turned their machines and fled south and when the machines would no longer bear them in the sky they landed in a narrow desert valley. And after a time they took to wife the women of that country. So did my tribe spring forth—

"On the fringes of the desert, life is very hard, but my people learned to use the waste for what it will give man and later they held much good land. Until twice twelve moons ago did they hold it—then the earth trembled and shook so that a man could not stand upright. From the mountains to our southland came fire and many evil smells. Talu of the Long Beard and Mack the Three Fingered died of coughing in the death fog which came down upon the village. And in the morning the world shook again just as the dawn light broke and this time the mountains spewed forth burning rock which flowed down to engulf the best of our hard-won fields and pastures. So we gathered what we might and fled before it, all the tribe together, driving our sheep and taking with us only what might be carried in the pony carts and on our backs.

"We struck to the north and discovered that the earth had broken in other places also so that to the east the sea had eaten into the land. Then we must flee from the rising waters as we had fled from the fire. And it seemed that nowhere might we find a place to call our own again. Until at last we came into this territory where so many of the Old Ones once had lived. Then divers of the young warriors, myself among them, were sent on to scout and mark out fields for our sowing and a place to build anew the Village of Birds. This is a fair country—" Arskane's hand gestured south. "I saw much and should have returned with my news, but, having come so far, my heart would not let me rest until I saw more and more of its wonders. I watched in secret the comings and goings of the Plainspeople, but they are not as my folk. It is in their hearts to live in houses of skin which may be set up in any field they choose and taken down again when they grow weary. Your mountain breed I do not know—we have little liking for high places since our mountains brought destruction upon us.

"These cities of the dead have their uses. One can find treasures here—as you know well. One can also find worse things." He touched the bandage pad on his shoulder. "I do not think my people will have a liking for the cities. Now, when I can again walk a straight trail, I must go back to report to the tribe. And maybe it shall follow that we will settle along some river valley where the soil is black and rich. And there shall we open up old fields to the seed grain, and turn out our sheep to graze on the hillsides. Then shall the Village of Birds again take root, in a fair and fruitful land." He sighed.

"You have named yourself a warrior," Fors said slowly. "Against whom do you war? Are there Beast Things also in your deserts?"

Arskane smiled grimly. "In the days of the Great Blow-up the Old Ones loosed certain magic they could not control. Our wise ones know not the secret, having only to guide them the tales of our fathers, the flying men. But this magic acted in strange and horrible ways. There were things in the desert which were born enemy to man, scaled creatures most horrible to look upon. The magic made these both cunning and quick so that it was ever war to the death between them and all humankind. But as yet they seem few and perhaps the molten rock from the mountains has eaten them up entirely. For we have seen none of their breed since we left."

"Radiation." Fors played with the hilt of his short sword. "Radiation mutations—but sometimes it worked well. Lura's kind was born of such magic!"

The dark-skinned southerner looked at the cat who sprawled at ease beyond. "That was good—not evil—magic. I wish that my people had friends such as that to protect them in their wanderings. For we have had to fight many times against beasts and men. The Plainspeople have not shown themselves friends to us. There is always danger to watch for. One night when I was in a dead place I was set upon by a pack of nightmare creatures. Had I not been able to climb beyond their reach and use my knife well they would have stripped the flesh from my bones."

"That I know." Fors brought out the drum and put it into the other's hands and Arskane gave a little cry of pure delight.

"Now can I talk with the Master of Scouts!" His fingers

started to tap out a complicated beat on the head but Fors' hand shot out and clamped about his wrist.

"No!" The mountaineer forced the fingers away from the drum. "That might signal others—as well as your people. It was a thing unknown to me which dug that trap—"

The scowl which twisted Arskane's black brows smoothed away as the mountaineer continued:

"I believe that that is the work of the Beast Things. And if they still skulk in this city your drum would bring them in—"

"The trap was old—"

"Yes. But never yet have we found Beast Things living together in great numbers. He who set it may now be still dwelling only the length of these ruins from us. This is a large city and all the men of the Eyrie would not be enough to search it well."

"Your tongue is as straight as your wit." Arskane set aside the drum. "We shall get free of this dwelling place of shadows before I try to speak with the tribe. Tomorrow I shall be able to take the trail. Let us be off with the dawn light. There is an evil in these old places which seems to clog the nostrils. I like better the cleanness of the open land."

Fors made up a small bundle of the city loot, caching what remained in an inner room. His leg was fully healed and Arskane could ride the mare for the next day or two. Regretfully the mountaineer looked upon the pile of his gleanings before he covered them up. But at least he had the map he had made and the journal of his explorations both packed away in the Star pouch, along with some of the colored pencils and the small figures from the museum case.

Arskane wandered through the building most of the afternoon, trying his legs he said, but also interested in what lay there. Now he turned on one wrist a wide band of wrought gold and carried a massive club with the head of a spike embedded in a ball which he had found in a room devoted to implements of war. His throwing spears and bow had been recovered from the depths of the trap but the shafts of the spears were broken and he could not draw the bow until his shoulder healed.

The sultry heat of the past days had not yet closed in when they ate their last meal in the museum at dawn the next day and stamped out the fire. Arskane protested against riding but Fors argued him up on the mare and they started out along the one trail the mountaineer had mapped, the one which had brought him into the city. They made no stops, traveling at their best pace down the littered street—with before them the cluster of tall buildings which had been Fors' goal on his first day in the city. If fortune favored them he was sure they could be almost out of the circle of the ruins by nightfall.

Arskane used his hands as sun shields and watched with wonder the towering buildings they moved among.

"Mountains—man made—that is what we see here. But why did the Old Ones love to huddle together in such a fashion? Did they fear their own magic so that they must live cheek to cheek with their kind lest it eat them up when it was loosed—as it did? Well, they died of it in the end, poor Old Ones. And now we have a better life—"

"Do we?" Fors kicked at a loose stone. "They had such knowledge—we are groping in the dark for only crumbs of what they knew—"

"But they did not use all their learning for good!" Arskane indicated the ruins. "This city came out of their brains and then it was also destroyed by them. They built only to tear down again. I think it better to build than to blast."

As the murmur of his words died away Fors' head snapped around. He had caught a whisper of sound, a faint pattering. And had he, or had he not, seen the loathsome outline of a bloated rat body slipping into a shat-

tered window? There were sounds among the stones
—almost as if some thing—or things—were following
them.

Lura's ears were flat to her skull, her eyes only battle
slits in her brown mask. She stood with her forepaws
planted upon a fallen column staring back along the track
they had come, the tip of her tail quivering.

Arskane caught their unease.

"What is—"

At first Fors thought that the scream which answered
that half question came from the throat of a bird. And
then the mare swung up her head and gave a second wild
cry. Arskane threw himself off just as she reared to crash
back on the stones. Then Fors saw the dart rising and
falling in the gaping wound which had torn open her
throat.

"In—!" Arskane's hand about his wrist jerked him into
a cavern opening in the front of the highest tower. As
they fled Lura's blood-chilling war cry ripped the air. But
a second later she too was with them pushing back into
the dark center of the building.

They paused at the top of a ramp which led down into
murky shadows. There were floors below. Fors could see
a bit of them. But Arskane pointed to the floor. Beaten in
the dust and dried mud was a regular path of footprints—made by feet too narrow—clawed feet!

Lura backed away from that highway spitting and snarling. So—they had not escaped but come straight into the
stronghold of the enemy! And it did not need the cry of
triumph from without, coming in shrill inhuman exultation, to confirm that.

But the trail led down—they might still go up! Lura
and Arskane shared Fors' thought, for both ran for the
left hand corridor which was parallel to the street level.
There were heavy doors along the hall, and no matter
how hard they pushed none of these gave. Only one at
the very end was open and they crowded up to look down

a shaft into utter darkness. But Fors had glimpsed something else.

"Hold my belt!" he ordered Arskane. "There is something to the left—"

With the southerner's fingers hooked in his belt he dared to swing over the edge of the opening. He was right, a ladder of metal strips protruded from the wall. And when he looked up he could see a square of dull light above which must mean another open door maybe a floor or two above. But could Lura and Arskane climb too?

Arskane flexed his arms as Fors explained, testing his shoulder.

"How far above is the opening?" he wanted to know.

"Perhaps two floors—"

While they hesitated Lura edged to the lip of the shaft, measured with her eyes the reach to the ladder, and then was gone before Fors could stop her. They heard the rasp of her claws on the metal—a sound to be drowned out by another—a shuffling noise of many feet. The inhabitants of the lower depths were issuing out to hunt. Arskane tested the lashing which held his war club to his belt. Then he smiled—if a bit crookedly.

"Two floors should not be beyond my strength. And we can only try, my friend."

He judged his distance as the cat had done and then swung away. With a pounding heart Fors waited where he was, not daring to watch that ascent. But the sound he dreaded most to hear—that of a falling body—did not follow. He fitted an arrow to his bow cord and waited.

And that wait was not long. A grayish shadow at the far corner of the corridor was target enough. He shot, pinning the gray patch to the wall with the steel-headed war arrow. Something screeched and tried to jerk free. But before it did Fors had shouldered his bow and had pushed off for the ladder. The strips remained firm under his weight—his minor nightmare had been their breaking loose after taking the strain of the cat and the big southerner—and he scrambled up at a furious pace, his breathing sounding a hurricane in his own ears. He pulled himself through that other gray space to find Lura and Arskane both anxiously waiting for him.

They were in a second corridor fronted by rows of doors, but some of these were already open. Arskane disappeared through the nearest while Fors lay belly down on the floor, his head at the opening of the shaft, listening to the sounds from below. The wailing of the thing he had wounded faded away but the shuffling noise was louder and there were growls which might or might not have been speech. So far the creatures below had not discovered how the quarry had fled.

Fors scrambled to his feet and caught at the door which had once closed the shaft—now it stood a few inches out from where it slid into the wall. Under his tugging it gave a little with a faint grating sound. The mountaineer exerted his full strength and gained a foot more.

But the grating must have betrayed them. There was a shout below and a dart sped up the shaft, to spin harmlessly back again. Arskane came up pushing before him a collection of moldering furniture.

Odd noises arose from the shaft but Fors was not tricked into looking over the edge. He continued his silent struggle with the door. Arskane stood to help him. Together they fought the stubborn metal, salt sweat stung in their eyes and dripped from their chins.

In the shaft the sounds grew louder. Several more darts skimmed into the light and fell. One, aimed with more skill or luck, skidded out across the floor between Fors' feet. Arskane turned to his erection of furniture and gave it one mighty push, toppling the whole pile over. There was a terrified yell in answer and a distant crash. Arskane rubbed a dusty hand across his wet jaw.

"One of them, by the Horned Lizard, climbs no more!"

They had the door halfway across the shaft opening now. And all at once its resistance ended with a snap which almost sent them both flying. Fors cried out triumphantly—but too soon. A foot was all they had gained. There still remained open space enough for a body to squeeze through.

Arskane drew off and considered the door for a long moment. Then he slapped it with the flat of his hand, putting behind that blow all the force he could muster. Again it gave and came forward a few inches. But the sounds in the shaft had begun again. The hunters had not been deterred by the fate of their companion.

Something flipped out of the dark, landing close to Fors' foot. It was a hand, but skeleton thin and covered with wrinkled grayish skin. As it scrabbled with twisted claws for a hold it seemed more a rat's paw than a hand. Fors raised his foot and stamped, grinding the boot, nailed to cross mountain trails, into the very center of the monstrosity. The scream which answered that came from the mouth of the shaft. They threw themselves in a last furious attack upon the door, their nails breaking and tearing on the metal—and it gave—snapping into the groove awaiting it in the opposite wall.

For a long moment they leaned panting against the wall of the corridor, holding their bruised and bleeding hands out before them. Fists were beating against that door but it did not move.

"That will stay closed," Arskane gasped at last. "They cannot hang upon the wall ladder and force it. If there is no other way up we are safe—for a time—"

Lura came down the hallway, threading her way in and out of the rooms along it. And there was no menace there. They would have a breathing spell. Or were they now caught in a trap as cruel as the one which had engulfed Arskane in the museum wood?

The southerner turned to the front of the building and Fors followed him to one of the tall windows, long bare of glass, which gave them sight of the street below. They could see the body of the mare but the pack she had car-

ried had been stripped off and there was something queer
about the way she lay—

"So—they are meat eaters—"

Fors gagged at Arskane's words. The mare was
meat—maybe they, too, were—meat! He raised sick eyes
and saw that the same thought lay in the big man's mind.
But Arskane's hand was also on the club he had taken
from the museum.

"Before this meat goes into any pot, it will have to be
taken. And the hunting of it is going to cost them sore.
These are truly the Beast Things of which you have spoken, comrade?"

"I believe so. And they are reputed to be crafty—"

"Then must we, too, be sly. Now, since we cannot go
down—let us see what may lie above us."

Fors watched the pigeons wheeling about the ruins.
The floor under their feet was white with bird droppings.

"We have no wings—"

"No—but I am bred of a race which once flew," Arskane answered with a sort of quiet humor coloring his
tone. "We shall find a way out of here that that offal below cannot follow. Let us now seek it."

They passed out of one hall into another, looking into
the rooms along the way. Here were only decaying sticks
of furniture and bones. In the third hall were more of the
shaft doors—all closed. Then, in the far end of one back
hall, Arskane pushed open a last door and they came
upon stairs which led both up and down.

Lura brushed past them and went down, fading away
with her customary skill and noiselessness. They squatted
down in the shadows to wait her report.

Arskane's face showed a grayish tinge which was not
born of the lack of light. The struggle up that ladder and
with the door had left its marks on him. He grunted and
settled his bad shoulder gingerly against the wall. Fors
edged forward. Now that they were quiet his ears could
work for him. He heard the pattering which was Lura on

her way, the trickle of powdered rubble which her paws
had disturbed somewhere.

There was no sign hereabout that the Beast Things had
used this stair. But—Lura had stopped! Fors closed his
eyes, blanking out his own thoughts, trying as he never
had before to catch the emanations of the big cat's mind.
She was not in any danger but she was baffled. The path
before her was closed in such a manner that she could not
win through. And when her brown head appeared again
above the top step Fors knew that they could not escape
by that route. He said as much to Arskane.

The tall man pulled himself to his feet with a weary
sigh.

"So. Then let us climb—but gently, comrade. These
stairs of the Old Ones beat a man's breath out of his
body!"

Fors pulled Arskane's arm over his shoulder, taking
some of the weight of the larger man.

"Slow shall it be—we have the full day before us—"

"And perhaps the night, too, and some other days.
Well, climb—comrade."

Five floors higher Arskane sank down, pulling Fors
with him. And the mountaineer was glad of the rest. They
had gone slowly, to be sure, but now his leg ached and his
breath sobbed in a band of pain beneath his small ribs.

For a space they simply sat there, taking deep breaths
and resting. Then Fors noticed with dismay that the sunlight was fading in the patches on the floor. He crawled to
a window and looked out. Through the jagged teeth of
broken buildings he could see the waters of the lake and
the sun was far into the west. It must be late afternoon.

Arskane shook himself awake at that information.

"Now we come," he observed, "to the matter of food.
And perhaps we have too often refreshed ourselves from
your canteen—"

Water! Fors had forgotten that. And where inside this
maze would they find either food or drink? But Arskane

was on his feet now and going through the door which must lead to the rest of that floor. Birds— Fors remembered the evidences of their nesting here—that would be the answer—birds!

But they came into a long room where some soft fabric lay under their feet. There were many tables set in rows down its length, each encircled by chairs. Fors caught the glint of metal laid out in patterns on the nearest. He picked up an unmistakable fork! This then had been an eating place of the Old Ones. But the food—any food would be long since gone.

He said that aloud only to have Arskane shake his head.

"Not so, comrade. Rather do I say that we are favored with such luck as few men have. In my journey north I chanced upon just such a place as this and in the smaller rooms behind I found many jars of food left by the Old Ones, but still good. That night did I feast as might a chieftain when the Autumn Dances begin—"

"To eat food found in the old places is to choose death. That is the law!" repeated Fors stubbornly. But he did trail along behind as Arskane moved purposely toward the door at the other end of the room.

"There are foods of many kinds. This I can reason— the container which holds it must be perfect—without blemish. Even I, who have not the lore of these dead places, can guess that. But I live, do I not, and I have eaten of the bounty left by the Old Ones. We can do no less than seek for it here."

Arskane, wise from his earlier experience, brought them into a room where shelves stood around the walls. Jars of glass and metal containers were arranged in rows along the shelves and Fors marveled at the abundance. But the southerner walked slowly around, peering intently at the glass jars, paying no attention to the metal red with rust. He came back at last with a half dozen bottles in his arms and put them down on the table in the center of the room.

"Look well at the topping, comrade. If you see no signs of decay there, then strike it off and eat!"

Ten minutes later they were sucking sticky fingers, gorged on fruit which had been there for generations before their birth. The juice appeased their thirst and Fors listened to sounds from the rooms ahead. Lura feasted too—so birds did nest here.

Arskane used his belt knife to snap the top from another jar.

"We need not worry for our food. And tomorrow we shall discover a way out of here. For once the Beast Things of the dead places have found their match!"

And Fors, gorged and content, met that confidence with his own.

8

Where Once Men Flew—

THEY SLEPT FITFULLY THAT NIGHT on piles of moldering fabrics they dragged together, and on rousing ate and drank again from the supplies in the storeroom. Then they climbed once more until the steps ended in a platform which had once been walled by large glass windows. Below the city spread out in all its broken glory. Fors identified the route he had pioneered on entering and pointed it out. And Arskane did the same for the one he had followed in the east.

"South should be our road now—straight south—"

Fors laughed shortly at that observation.

"We have yet to win free of this one building," he objected. But Arskane was ready with an answer to that.

"Come!" One of his big hands cupped the mountaineer's shoulder as he drew Fors to the empty window space facing east. Far below lay the broad roof of a neighbor building, its edge tight against the side of the tower.

"You have this." Arskane flipped the end of the mountain rope still wrapping Fors' belt. "We must go down to those windows just above that roof and swing through to it. See, south lies a road of roofs across which we may travel for a space. These Beast Things may be cunning but perhaps they do not watch the sky route against escape—it hangs above the ways they seem to like best. It is in my mind that they hug the ground on their journeyings—"

"It is said that they best love to slink in the burrows," confirmed Fors. "And they are supposed to be none too fond of the open light of day—"

Arskane plucked his full lower lip between forefinger and thumb. "Night fighters—eh? Well then, day is the time for us—the light is in our favor."

They made the long climb down with lighter hearts. A story above the neighboring roof they found a window in the center of the hallway which faced in the right direction, broke out the few splinters of glass still set dagger-wise in the frame, and leaned out to reconnoiter.

"The rope will not be needed after all," Arskane commented. "That drop is easy." He took a strong grip on the window frame and flexed his muscles.

Fors crossed to the next window and set an arrow on his bow cord. But, as far as he could see, the roof below, the silent blank windows were empty of menace. Only— he could not cover all of those. And death might fly from any one of the hundreds of black holes, above, below—

But this was their best—maybe their only chance of escape. Arskane grunted with pain from his shoulder. Then he was out, tumbling down to the surface below. As quickly as he had taken the leap he dodged behind the high parapet.

For a long moment they both waited, frozen. Then, in a flash of brown and cream, Lura went through, making a more graceful landing. She sped across the roof, a streak of light fur.

So far—so good. Fors freed himself from quiver, Star Man's pouch, and bow, tossing them through in the general direction of Arskane. Then he hoisted himself on the sill and swung. He heard Arskane's shout of warning just as he let go. Startled, he could not prepare for a proper landing but fell hard—with a force which jarred him.

He squirmed over on his back. A dart quivered in the frame of the window where his hand had rested. He rolled into the safety of the parapet with a force which brought him up with a crack against Arskane's knees.

"Where did that come from?"

"There!" The southerner pointed at the row of windows in the building across the street. "From one of those—"

"Let us go—"

Belly flat, Fors started a snake's progress toward the opposite end of the roof. They could not go back now— to try to climb up to that window would be to present a target which even a fumbling marksman could not miss. But now the hunt was on and they would have to make a running fight of it through a maze which the enemy knew intimately and they did not know at all—a maze which might be studded with traps more subtle and more cruel than the one which had imprisoned Arskane—

A thin fluting—like the piping of a child's reed whistle—cut the air somewhere behind. Fors guessed it to be what he had dreaded most to hear—the signal that the quarry had been flushed out of hiding and was now to be pursued in the open.

Arskane had forged ahead. And because the big man seemed to know just what he was going to do next Fors accepted his lead. They came into a corner of the parapet between the east and south sides of the roof. Lura had already gone over it; she called softly from below.

"Now we must trust to luck, comrade—and to the favor of Fortune. Slip over quickly on the same instant that I move. It may be that if we give them two targets they will not be able to choose either. Are you ready?"

"Yes!"

"Then—go!"

Fors reached up and caught the top of the parapet at the same moment Arskane moved. Together their bodies went over and they let themselves roll across the second roof, painfully shedding some skin in the process. Here the surface was not clear. Blocks, fallen from a taller building beyond, made a barrier which Arskane greeted with an exclamation of satisfaction. Both gained the protection of the rubble and squatted down to listen. The pipe of the whistle sounded again, imperatively. Arskane rubbed dust off his hands.

"Beyond here lies another street, and below is the river valley which you crossed—"

Fors nodded. He, too, could remember what they had seen from the tower. The river valley made a curve, cutting due east at this point. He shut his eyes for an instant the better to visualize the old train yards, the clustered buildings—

"Well," Arskane shook himself, "if we give them more time they will be better able to greet us in a manner we shall not relish. Therefore, we must keep on the move. Now that they expect to find us on roof tops it might be wise to seek the street level—"

"See here." Fors had been examining the rubbish about them. "This did not fall from above." He dug into the pile of rubble. Set in the roof was a slanted door. Arskane pounced upon it joyfully.

They dug as furiously as ground squirrels in autumn until they cleared it. Then they tugged it open and looked down into a musty darkness from which old evil odors arose. There were stairs, almost ladder steep. They used them.

Long hallways and more stairs. Although all three walked with the silence of forest hunters their passing sent small thuds and old sighings through the deserted building. Now and again they stopped to listen. But Lura manifested no signs of uneasiness and Fors could hear nothing beyond the fall of plaster, the shifting of old boards their tread had disturbed.

"Wait!" He caught Arskane as the latter started down the last flight of stairs. Fors' swinging hand had struck lightly against a door in the wall and something in the hollow sound which had followed that blow seemed promising. He opened the door. They stepped out on a kind of ledge above a wide cavern of a place.

"By the Great Horned Lizard!" Arskane was shaken and Fors gripped the rail which framed the platform.

They looked down into what once must have been a storage place for the heavy trucks which the Old Ones had used for transportation of goods. Ten—fifteen of the monsters stood in line waiting for the masters who were long gone. And several were of the sealed engine type which had been the last invention of the Old Ones. These appeared unblighted by time, still perfect and ready for use.

One of them had its nose almost against a wide closed door. A door, decided Fors instantly, which must give upon the street. A wild idea began to flower in his mind. He turned to Arskane.

"There was a road leading down into the valley of the trains—a road which was mostly steep slope—"

"True—"

"See that machine—the one by the gate? If we could start it out it would roll down that street and nothing could stop it!"

Arskane licked his lips. "The machine is probably dead. Its motor would not run and we could not push it—"

"We might not need to push. And do not be sure that the motor would not serve us. Jarl of the Star Men once piloted a sealed motor car a full quarter of a mile before it died again. If this would only bring us to the top of the slope it would be enough. At least we can try. It would be a safe and easy way to gain the valley—"

"As you say—we can try!" Arskane bounded down the steps and headed for the truck.

The door to the driver's seat hung open as if to welcome them. Fors slid across the disintegrating pad to sit behind the controls—just as if he were one of the Old Ones who had used this marvel as a matter of course.

Arskane crowded in beside him and was leaning forward to examine the rows of dials and buttons confronting them. He touched one.

"This locks the wheels—"

"How do you know?"

"We have a man of learning in the tribe. He has taken apart many of the old machines to learn the secret of their fashioning. Only we have no longer the fuel to run them and so they are of no use to us. But from Unger I have learned something concerning their powers."

Fors yielded his place, not without some reluctance, and watched Arskane delicately test the controls. At last the southerner stamped with his foot upon a floor-set button and what they had believed in their hearts would never happen, did. The ancient engine came to life. The sealed engine was not dead!

"The door!" Arskane's face was white beneath its brown stain, he clung to the wheel with real fear of the terrifying power that was throbbing under him.

Fors leaped out of the cab and dashed for the big door. He pulled down on the counter bar and it gave so that he could push back the ponderous barrier. He looked out upon a street clear of wrecks. A glance up slope told him why. At the head—only a few feet back from the door—one of the great trucks had slewed sidewise, its nose smashed into the wall of a building on the opposite side—an effective barricade. He did not linger after that fleeting examination. Behind, the sound of the dying engine was horrible—grating and grinding out its last few seconds of life.

Fors gained the cabin, bringing Lura in with him. They

crouched together with pounding hearts as Arskane fumbled with the wheel. But the last spurt of power set the big truck moving, rubber shredding away from the remains of the tires as they turned. The engine faltered and died as they rolled out of the garage and reached the rise, but the momentum carried on and they sped faster and faster down the steep hill to the valley below.

Only pure luck had given them that clear street ahead. Had it not been for the smashed truck corking the street at its head they might have crashed into wreckage which would have killed them all. Arskane fought the wheel, steering only by instinct, and brought them along the pavement at a pace which grew ever wilder as the truck gained speed.

Twice Fors closed his eyes only to force them open again. His hands were buried deep in the fur of the squalling Lura who wanted none of this form of travel. But the truck went on and on and they were at last on level land, bumping over the rusted tracks of the railroad. The truck slowed, and at last it stopped as it buried its front bumper in a heap of coal.

For a moment the three simply remained where they were, shaken and weak. Then they roused enough to tumble out. Arskane laughed, but his voice was going up scale as he said:

"If anyone followed us they must be well behind now. And we must labor so that such a distance grows even wider."

They took advantage of any cover afforded by the wreckage in the train yards, and struck south at a trotting pace until, at last, the valley of the river looped away again from the southern path they had set themselves. Then they climbed the slope and went on across the tree-grown ruins of the city outskirts.

The sun was overhead, hot on head and shoulders. There was a fishy scent in the breeze which blew inland from the lake. Arskane sniffed it loudly.

"Rain," was his verdict, "and we could not hope for better fortune. It will cover our trail—"

But the Beast Things would not follow any prey out of a city—or would they? They must be ranging farther afield now—there was that track left by the deer hunter. And Fors' father had been brought down by a pack, not within a city but in the fringes of the true forest land. It was not well to count themselves safe merely because they were drawing out of the ruined area.

"At least we travel without the weight of baggage," Arskane observed some time later as they paused to rest and drink the thick juice with which Fors had filled the canteen that morning.

Fors thought regretfully of the mare and the plunder which she had carried only yesterday. Not much remained now to prove his story—just the two rings on his fingers, and the few small things in the Star pouch. But he had the map and his travel journal to turn out before the Council when he had that accounting with the Eyrie which he thirsted for.

Arskane had even less than the mountaineer. The museum club in his hand was the only weapon he still had left except his belt knife. In his pouch he carried flint and steel, two fishhooks and a line wound about them.

"If we but had the drum," he regretted. "Were that in my hand we should even now be talking with my people. Without signals it will be a chancy matter to find them—unless we cross the trail of another scout."

"Come with me—to the Eyrie!" Fors said impulsively.

"When you told me your story, comrade, did you not say that you fled your tribe? Will they be quicker to welcome you back with a stranger at your heels? This is a world in which hate lives yet. Let me tell you of my own people—this is a story of the old, old days. The flying men who founded my tribe were born with dark skins—and so they had in their day endured much from those born of fairer races. We are a people of peace but there is an ancient hurt behind us and sometimes it stirs in our memories to poison with bitterness.

"As we moved north we strove to make friends with the Plainspeople—three times that I have knowledge of did we send heralds unto them. And each time were we greeted by a flight of war arrows. So now we have hardened our hearts and we stand for ourselves if the need be. Can you promise that those of the mountains will hold out friendly hands if we seek them out?"

Hot blood stung Fors' cheeks. He was afraid that he knew the answer to that question. Strangers were ene-mies—that was the old, old ruling. Yet should it be so? This land was wide and rich and men were few. Surely there was enough of it for all—it went on and on to the sea. And in the old days men had fashioned ships and sailed across seas to other wide lands.

He said as much aloud and Arskane gave hearty and swift agreement.

"You reason with straight thoughts, comrade. Why should there be distrust between the twain of us because our skin differs in color and our tongues sound different to the ear? My people live by tilling the land, they plant seed and food grows from it, they herd sheep from which comes the wool to weave our wind cloaks and night cov-erings. We make jars and pots from clay and fire them into stone hardness, working with our hands and delight-ing in it. The Plainspeople are hunters, they have famed horses and run the herds of cattle—they love to keep ever moving—to know far trails. And your people—?"

Fors screwed his eyes against the sun. "My people? We are but a small tribe of few clans and often in the winter we needs must go lean and hungry for the mountains are a hard country. But above all do we love knowledge, we live to loot the ruins, to try to understand and relearn the things which made the Old Ones great in their time. Our medicine men fight against the ills of the bodies, our teachers and Star Men against the ignorance of the mind—"

"And yet these same people who fight ignorance have made of you a wandering one because you differ from them—"

For the second time Fors' skin burned red. "I am mutant. And mutant stock is not to be trusted. The—the Beast Things are also mutant—" He could not choke out more than that.

"Lura is mutant also—"

Fors blinked. The four quiet words of that answer meant more than just a statement of fact. The tenseness went out of him. He was warm, and not with shame, nor with the sun which was beating down on him. It was a good warmness he had not remembered feeling before—ever.

Arskane propped his chin on his hand and stared out over the tangle of bush and vine. "It seems to me," he said slowly, "that we are like the parts of one body. My people are the busy hands, fashioning things by which life may be made easier and more beautiful. The Plainspeople are the restless, hurrying feet, ever itching for new trails and the strange things which might lie beyond the sunrise and the sunset. And your clan is the head, thinking, remembering, planning for feet and hands. Together—"

"Together," Fors breathed, "we would make such a nation as this land has not seen since the days of the Old Ones!"

"No, not a nation such as the Old Ones knew!" Arskane's answer was sharp. "They were not one body—for they knew war. And out of that warfare came what is today. If the body grows together again it must be because each part, knowing its own worth and taking pride in it, recognizes also the worth of the other two. And color of skin, or eyes, or the customs of a man's tribe must mean no more to strangers when meeting than the dust they wash from their hands before they take meat. We must come to one another free of such dust—or it will rise to blind our eyes and what the Old Ones started will continue to live for ever and ever to poison the earth."

"If that could only be—"

"Brother," for the first time Arskane used the more intimate word to Fors, "my people believe that all the actions in this life have behind them some guiding power. And it seems to me that we two were brought to this place so that we might meet thus. And from our meeting perhaps there will be born something stronger and mightier that what we have known before. But now we linger here too long, death may still sniff at our heels. And it is not to my mind that we shall be turned from the path marked out for us."

Something in the solemn tones of the big man's voice reached into Fors. He had never had a real friend, his alien blood had set him too far apart from the other boys of the Eyrie. And his relationship with his father had been that of pupil with teacher. But he knew now that he would never willingly let this dark-skinned warrior go out of his life again, and that where Arskane chose to go, there he would follow.

When the sun was almost overhead they were in a wilderness of trees where it was necessary to go slowly to avoid gaping cellar holes and lengths of moldering beams. But in this maze Lura picked up the trail of a wild heifer and within the hour they had brought it down and were broiling fresh meat. With enough for perhaps two more meals packed in the raw hide they went on, Fors' small compass their guide.

Abruptly they came out on the edge of the old place of flying men. So abruptly they were almost shocked into dodging back into the screen of trees when they first saw what lay there.

Both were familiar with the pictures of such machines. But here they were real, standing in ordered rows—some of them. And the rest were piled in battered confusion, torn and rent or half engulfed in shell holes.

"Planes!" Arskane's eyes gleamed. "The sky-riding planes of my fathers' fathers! Before we fled the shaking of the mountains we went to look our last upon the ones which brought the first men of our clan to that land—and they were like unto some of these. But here is a whole field of planes!"

"These were struck dead before they reached the sky," Fors pointed out. A queer feeling of excitement burned inside him. The ground machines, even the truck which had helped them out of the city, never moved him so. These winged monsters—how great—how very great in knowledge must the Old Ones have been! That they could ride among the clouds in these—where now their sons must crawl upon the ground! Hardly knowing what he did Fors ventured out and drew his hand sadly along the body of the nearest plane. He was so small beside it—a whole family clan might have once ridden in its belly—

"It was with such as these that the Old Ones sowed death over the world—"

"But to ride in the clouds," Fors refused Arskane's somber mood, "above the earth— They must have been godlike—the Old Ones!"

"Say rather devil-like! See—" Arskane took him by the arm and led him between the two orderly rows on the edge of the field to look at the series of ragged, ugly craters which made a churned mess of the center of the airport. "Death came thus from the air, and men dropped that death willingly upon their fellows. Let us remember that, brother."

They passed around the wreckage, following the line of unwrecked planes until their way led to a building. There were many bones here. Many men had died trying to get the machines into the air—too late.

When they reached the building, both turned and looked back at the path of destruction and the two lines of curiously untouched bombers still waiting. The sky they would never again travel was clear and blue with small, clean-cut white clouds drifting across it in patterns. In the west other and darker clouds were gathering. A storm was in the making.

"This," Arskane pointed down the devastated field, "must never happen again. No matter what heights our sons rise to—we must not tear the earth against each other— Do you agree, brother?"

Fors met those dark burning eyes squarely. "It is agreed. And what I can do, that I shall. But—where men once flew they must fly again! That also we must swear to!"

9

Into the Blow-Up Land

FORS HUNCHED OVER THE TABLE, leaning on his elbows, hardly daring to breathe lest the precious cloth-backed squares he was studying crumble into powdery dust. Maps—such a wealth of maps he had never dreamed of. He could put finger tip to the point of blue which was the edge of the great lake—and from that he could travel across—straight to the A-T-L-A-N-T-I-C Ocean. Why, that was the fabulous sea! He looked up impatiently as Arskane came into this treasure room.

"We are here—right here!"

"And here we are like to stay forever if we do not bestir ourselves—"

Fors straightened up. "What—?"

"I have but come from the tower at the end of this building. Something alive moves at the far end of the field of machines. It is a shadow but it slides with too much purpose to be overlooked by a cautious—"

"A deer," began Fors, knowing that it was not.

Arskane gave a short bark of humor-lacking laughter. "Does a deer creep upon its belly and spy around corners, brother? No, I think that our friends from the city have

105

found us out at last. And I do not like being caught in this place—no, I do not like that at all!"

Fors left the maps regretfully. How Jarl would have delighted in them. But to attempt to move them would be to destroy them and they would have to remain—as they had through the countless years. He picked up his quiver and checked the remaining arrows. Only ten left. And when they were gone he would have only short sword and hunting knife—

Arskane must have picked that thought right out of his companion's mind for now he was nodding. "Come." He went back to the flight of stairs which led them in a spiral up and up until they stood in a place that had once been completely walled with glass. "See there—and what do you make of that?"

The southerner stabbed a finger southeast. Fors picked out a queer scar in the vegetation there, a wide wedge of land where nothing grew. Under the sun the soil had a strange metallic gleam. He had seen the raw rocks of mountain gorges and the cleared land where the Old Ones had once had concrete surfaces, but this was different. In a land where trees and grass had reclaimed their own nothing green encroached upon the wedge.

"Desert—" was all he could suggest doubtfully. But there should be no deserts in this section of the country.

"That it is not! Remember, I am desert born and that is no natural wasteland such as I have ever known. It is something the like of which I have not stumbled upon in all my journeying!"

"Hush!" Fors' head snapped around. He was sure of that sound, the distant scrape of metal against metal. His eyes ran along the lines of the silent machines. And there was a flicker of movement halfway down the second line!

He screened his eyes against the sun, crowding up to the frame of the vanished glass. Under the shadow of the spreading wing of a plane squatted a gray-black blot. And it was sniffing the ground!

His whisper hardly rose above the rasp of Arskane's quick breathing. "Only one—"

"No. Look within the curve of that bush—to the right—"

Yes, the southerner was right. Against the green, one could see the bestial head. The Beast Things almost always hunted as a pack. It was too much to hope that this time they did not. Fors' hand dropped to his sword hilt.

"We must go!"

Arskane's sandals already thudded on the stairs. But before he left the tower Fors saw that gray thing dart forward from under the plane. And two more such lumps detached themselves from the covering of trees along the ruined runway, taking cover among the machines. The pack was closing in.

"We must keep to the open," Arskane warned. "If we can stay ahead and not allow them to corner us we shall have a fair chance."

There was another door out of the building, one which gave upon the other half of the field. Here was a maze of tangled wreckage. Shell holes pocked the runways; machines and defense guns had been blasted too. They swung around the sky-pointing muzzle of an anti-aircraft gun. And in the same instant the air was rent with a horrible screech, answered by Lura's snarl of rage. A thrashing tangle of fighting cat and her prey rolled out almost under their feet.

Arskane swung his club with a sort of detached science. He struck down, hard. Thin, bone-gray arms went wide and limp and Lura was clawing a dead body. A missile from the wreckage grazed Fors' head sending him spinning against the gun. He stumbled over the body from which came a filthy stench. Then Arskane jerked him to his feet and pulled him under the up-ended nose of a plane.

Still shaking his ringing head Fors allowed his companion to guide him as they turned and dodged. Once he heard the ring of metal as a Beast Thing dart struck. Arskane pushed him to the left, the momentum of the southerner's shove carrying both of them into cover.

"Driving us—" Arskane panted. "They herd us like deer—".

Fors tried to struggle free of the other's prisoning hand.

"Lura—ahead—" In spite of the blow which had rocked him he caught the cat's message. "There the way lies clear—"

Arskane did not seem disposed to leave cover but Fors tore free and wriggled through an opening in the churned earth and broken machines. It seemed to last hours, that crawling, twisting race with death. But in the end they came out on the edge of that queer scar in the earth which they had sighted from the tower. And there Lura crouched, her lips lifted in a snarl, her tail sweeping steadily to signify her rage.

"Down that gully—quick—" Arskane was into the notch before he had finished speaking.

The strange earth crunched under Fors' boots. He took the only way left to freedom. And Lura, still giving low voice to her dismay, swept by him.

Here there was not even moss and the rocky outcrops had a glassy glaze. Fors shrank from touching anything with his bare flesh. The sounds of pursuit were gone though. It was too quiet here. He realized suddenly that what his ears missed was the ever-present sound of insects which had been with them in the vegetation of the healthy world.

This country they had entered blindly was alien, with no familiar green and brown to meet the eye, no homely sounds for the reassurance of the ear. Arskane had paused and as Fors caught up he asked the question which was on his tongue tip.

"What is this place?"

But the southerner countered with a question of his own. "What have you been told of the Blow-Up Lands?"

"Blow-Up Lands?" Fors tried to remember the few

scanty references to such in the records of the Eyrie. Blow-Up Lands—where atom bombs had struck to bite into the earth's crust, where death had entered so deeply that generations must pass before man could go that way again—

His mouth opened and then shut quickly. He did not have to ask his question again. He knew—and the chill horror of that knowing was worse than a Beast Thing dart striking into his flesh. No wonder there had been no pursuit. Even the mutant Beast Things knew better than to venture here!

"We must go back—" he half whispered, already knowing that they could not.

"Go back to certain death? No, brother, and already it is too late. If the old tales be true we are even now walking dead men with the seeds of the burning sickness in us. Instead—if we go on—there is a chance of getting through—"

"Perhaps more than a chance." Fors' first horror faded as he recalled an old argument long ago worn to rags by the men of the Eyrie. "Tell me, Arskane, in the early years after the Blow-Up did the people of your tribe suffer from the radiation sickness?"

The big man's straight brows drew together. "Yes. There was a death year. All but ten of the clan died within three months. And the rest sickened and were ever weakly. It was not until a generation later that we grew strong again."

"So was it also with those of the Eyrie. Men of my clan who have studied the ancient books say that because of this sickness we are now different from the Old Ones who gave us birth. And perhaps because of that difference we may venture unharmed where death would have struck them down."

"But this reasoning has not yet been put to the proof?"

Fors shrugged. "Now it is. And we shall see if it is correct. I know that I am mutant."

"While I am like the others of my tribe. But that is not saying that they are the same as the Old Ones. Well, whether it be what we hope or not, we are set on this path. And there is truly death, and an unpleasant one, behind us. In the meantime—that is a storm coming. We had best find shelter, this is no land to blunder across in the dark!"

It was hard to keep one's footing on the greasy surface and Fors guessed that if it were wet it would be worse than sand to plow through. They held to the sides of the narrow valleys which laced the country, looking for a cave or overhang which would afford the slightest hint of shelter.

The dark clouds made a sullen gray mass and a premature twilight. A bad night to go without a fire—in the open of the contaminated land under a dripping sky.

A jagged flash of purple lightning cracked across the heavens and both of them shielded their eyes as it struck not far from where they stood. The rumble of the thunder which followed almost split their ear drums. Then the rain came in a heavy smothering curtain to close them in. They huddled together, miserable, the three of them against the side of a narrow valley, cowering as the lightning struck again and again and the water rose in a stream down the center of the gully, washing the soil from the glassy rocks. Only once did Fors move. He unhooked his canteen and pulled at Arskane's belt flask until the big man gave it to him. These he set out in the steady downpour. The water which ran by his feet was contaminated but the rain which had not yet touched soil or rock might be drinkable later.

Lura, Fors decided, must be the most unhappy of the three. The rain ran from their smooth skin and was not much held by their rags of clothing. But her fur was matted by it and it would take hours of licking with her tongue before it was in order again. However, she did not voice her disapproval of life as she usually did. Since they had crossed into the atom-blasted land she had not given tongue at all. On impulse Fors tried now to catch her thoughts. He had been able to do that in the past—just enough times to be sure that she could communicate when she wished. But now he met only a blank. Lura's wet fur pressed against him now, but Lura herself had gone.

And then he realized with a start that she was listening, listening so intently that her body was now only one big organ for the trapping of sound. Why?

He rested his forehead on his arms where he had crossed them on his hunched knees. Deliberately he set about shutting out the sounds around him—the drum of the rain, Arskane's breathing, the gurgle of the water threading by just beyond their toes. Luckily the thunder had stopped. He was conscious of the pounding of his own blood in his ears, of the hiss of his own breath. He shut them out, slowly, as thoroughly as he could. This was a trick he had tried before but never with such compulsion on him. It was very necessary now that he *hear*— and that warning might have come either from Lura or some depth within him. He concentrated to shut out even the drive of that urgency—for it too was a danger.

There was a faint plopping sound. His mind considered it briefly and rejected it for what it was—the toppling of earth undercut by the storm-born stream. He pushed the boundaries of his hearing farther away. Then, even as a strange dizziness began to close in, he heard it—a sound which was not born of the wind and the rain. Lura moved, rising to her feet. Now she turned and looked at him as he raised his head to meet her eyes.

"What—?" Arskane stirred uneasily, staring from one to the other.

Fors almost laughed at the blank bewilderment in the big man's eyes.

The dizziness which had come from his concentration was receding fast. His eyes adjusted to the night and the shadows. He got to his feet and put aside bow and quiver, keeping only the belt with his sword and knife. Arskane put out a protesting hand which he eluded.

"There is something back there. It is important that I see it. Wait here—"

But Arskane was struggling up too. Fors saw his mouth twist with pain as he inadvertently put weight upon his left arm. The rain must have got to the healing wound. And seeing that, the mountaineer shook his head.

"Listen—I am mutant—you have never asked in what manner I differ. But it is this, I can see in the dark—even this night is little different from the twilight for me. And my ears are close to Lura's in keenness. Now is the hour when my difference will serve us. Lura!" He swung around and looked for a second time deep into those startlingly blue eyes. "Here will you stay—with our brother. Him will you guard—as you would me!"

She shifted her weight from one front paw to another, standing up against his will in the recesses of her devious mind, refusing him. But he persisted. He knew her stubborn freedom and the will for it which was born into her kind. They called no man master and they went their own way always. But Lura had chosen him, and because he had no friends among his own breed they had been very close, perhaps closer than any of the Eyrie had been with the furred hunters before. Fors did not know how much she would yield to his will but this was a time when he must set himself against her. To leave Arskane here alone, handicapped by his wound and his lack of night sight, would be worse than folly. And the big man could not go with him. And the sound—that must be investigated!

Lura's head came up. Fors reached down his hand and felt the wetness of her fur as she rubbed her jaw along his fist in her most intimate caress. He had a moment of pure happiness at her acceptance of his wish. His fingers scratched behind her ears lovingly.

"Stay here," he told them both. "I shall return as quickly as I may. But we must know what lies there—"

Before he finished that sentence he was off, not giving either of them time to protest again, knowing that the rain and the darkness would hide him from Arskane within a few feet and that Lura would be on guard until his return.

Fors slipped and stumbled, splashing through small pools, following the route he had memorized as they came. The rain was slacking, it stopped entirely as he reached the top of a pinnacle of rock and looked out again over the old airport. He could distinguish the bombed section and the building where they had found the maps. But he was more interested in what was directly below.

There was no fire—although his mind kept insisting that there should be one, for it was plain that he was spying upon a council. The circle of hunched figures bore an uncanny and, to him, unwholesome resemblance to the meetings of the elders in the Eyrie. The Things were squatting so that their bodies were only blotches—for that he was glad. Somehow he had no desire to see them more clearly. But one pranced and droned in the center of that circle, and the sounds it uttered were what had drawn Fors there.

He could distinguish gutturals which must be words, but they had no meaning for him. Arskane's tongue and his own had once had a common base and it had not been difficult to learn each other's speech. But this growling did not sound as if it were shaped by either lips or brain which were human.

What the leader urged he could not know, but what they might do as a result of that urging was important. The Beast Things were growing bolder with the years. At first they had never ventured beyond the edges of the cities. But now they would follow a trail beyond the ruins and perhaps they were sending scouts into the open country. They were a menace to the remaining humans—

The leader ended his or its speech abruptly. Now its too thin body turned and it pointed to the wasteland where Fors crouched, almost as if it had sighted the hidden watcher. The gesture was answered by a growl from its companions. One or two got to their feet and padded to the edge of the Blow-Up ground where their heads sank as they sniffed warily at the polluted soil. But it did not take them long to make up their minds. For they were gathering up their bundles of darts and forming into a sort of crude marching line.

Fors stayed just long enough to be sure that they were indeed coming, that whatever taboo had held them back no longer operated. Then he fled, skimming lightly at his sure woods' pace, back to where he had left Lura and Arskane. The Beast Things did not seem too cheerful about their venture and their starting pace was slow. They walked as if they expected to find traps under their feet. There was hope that the pursued could keep ahead of them.

The mountaineer found Arskane impatient, Lura crouched on an outcrop, her eyes glowing in the dark. Fors grabbed up the equipment he had discarded as he gasped out his news.

"I have been thinking," Arskane's slower but deeper voice cut through his report. "We do not understand the weapons of the Old Ones, those which could make a desert such as this. Was there only one bomb which fell here, or were there more? But the heart of such a place would be more dangerous than its lip. If we head straight across we may be going to that death tradition promises for those who invade the blue places. But if we circle we may—"

"There is the matter of time. I tell you trackers run on our heels now."

"Yes, and they track by scent. There is at hand an answer to that."

Arskane's moccasins plowed through a pool, sending

up spray. Fors understood. The thread of stream might be their salvation after all. But, since the rain had ceased, the water was shrinking rapidly in volume, almost as if the rocky soil over which it ran was a sponge to suck it up.

Fors started ahead, his night sight picking out the pitfalls and bad footing for both of them. Sometimes it was only his hand which kept Arskane on his feet. The big man stumbled stubbornly on, his breath torn out of him in harsh gasps. Fors knew from the grip of cramp in his own leg muscles what tormented the other. But they must gain ground—gain it while the pursuers, still suspicious of the Blow-Up Land, traveled slowly.

Then, long after, Arskane fell and, although Fors allowed them both a rest, he could not get to his feet again. His head slumped forward on his chest and Fors saw that he was either unconscious or asleep, his mouth twisted with pain. But what was worse were the seeping stains on the bandage which still bound the wounded shoulder.

Fors pressed the palms of his hands against his burning eyes. He tried to think back—was it only last night they had slept in the city tower? It seemed a week behind them. They could not keep on at this rate, that was certain. Now that he relaxed against a sandy bank he was afraid he could not make the effort to get up again. He must sleep. And there was the matter of food also. How large was this Blow-Up desert? What if they must go on and on across it—maybe for days?

But they would be dead before days passed. Would it be better to choose a likely place now and make a last stand against the Beast Things? He dug his eyes again. He dared not sleep now. Then he remembered Lura.

She lay flat on a ridge a little above them, licking one paw, pausing now and then to prick her ears and listen. Lura would nap too, but in her own fashion, and nothing could come to attack while she watched. His head fell back against Arskane's limp arm and he slept.

10

✼ **Captured!**

THE GLARE OF SUN REFLECTED from the grease-slick surface of the bare rocks made Fors' eyes ache. It was hard to keep plodding steadily along when raw hunger gnawed at one's middle. But they had seen no game in this weird waste. And at the very worst he was not suffering as Arskane was. The southerner mumbled unintelligibly, his eyes were glazed, and it was necessary to lead him by the hand as if he were a tired child. The red stain on his bandaged shoulder was crusted and dried—at least he no longer lost blood he could ill afford to spare.

Where was the end of the Blow-Up country? If they had not traveled in circles they must have covered miles of its knife-edged valleys and rocky plateaus. And yet, still facing them at the top of each rise, was only more and more of the sick earth.

"Water—" Arskane's swollen tongue pushed across cracked lips.

All the abundance of yesterday's flood had vanished, absorbed in the soil as if it had never existed. Fors steadied the big man against a rock and reached for his

116

canteen. He did it slowly, trying to keep his hand from shaking. Not one precious drop must be spilled!

It was Arskane who did that. His eyes suddenly focused on the canteen and he grabbed for it. Water splashed over his hand and gathered in a depression of the stone. Fors looked at it longingly, but he still dared not swallow the fluid which had touched the tainted land here.

He allowed Arskane two swallows and then took the canteen away by force. Luckily the big man's strength had ebbed so that he could control him. As Fors fastened the canteen onto his belt he glanced at the ground. What he saw there kept him still and staring.

From out of the shadow cast by a rock something was moving toward the spilled water. It was dark green, mottled with reddish-yellow patches, and man's age-long distrust of a reptile almost made him send his boot crashing down on it. But in time he saw that it was not a snake that writhed across the ground, it was the long fleshy stem of a plant. Its flattened end wavered through the air and fell upon the water drops, arching over the moisture. Now the rest of the thing moved out to drink and Fors saw the three stiff leaves encircling a tall middle spike which bore a red bulb. The plant drank and the suckered stem lifted to curl back against the leaves as the whole fantastic growth withdrew into the shade, leaving the watcher to wonder if thirst and hunger had played tricks with his eyes. Only on the stone was a damp mark covering the hollow where the water had been.

So there was life here—even if it were an alien life. Somehow Fors was heartened by that glimpse of the plant. It was true that he was used to vegetation which remained rooted. But in a slice of land as strange as this men might well stay in place while the plants walked abroad. He laughed at that—it seemed a very witty and enlightening thought and he repeated it proudly to Arskane as they moved on. But the southerner answered only with a mumble.

The journey went on with the quality of a nightmare. Fors managed to keep going, pulling Arskane to his feet again and again, heading on to landmarks he established ahead. It was easier to keep moving if one picked out a rock or one of the slippery earth dunes and held to it as a guide. Then, when that point was achieved, there was always another ahead to fix on in the same manner.

He was sometimes aware of movement in the shadows which lay blue-black under rocks and ledges. Whether colonies of the water plants lurked there or other inhabitants of this hell who spied upon travelers, he neither knew nor cared. All that mattered was to keep going and hope that sometime when they topped one of the ridges they would sight the healthy green of their own world.

Now and then Lura came into sight, her once smooth fur rough and matted, her flanks shrunken and thin. Sometimes she would pad beside them for a few feet and then melt away on her own road, watchful and ready. If anything had found their back trail and was following it and them, it had not yet come within striking distance.

It was becoming almost impossible to keep Arskane going. Twice he would have fallen heavily full length if Fors had not steadied him, and the second time the collapse bore the mountaineer to his knees. It was then that he was reckless with the water, hoping to spur his companion on. And he did get the southerner to his feet. But now the canteen was empty.

They were struggling through a maze of knife-narrow ravines. But these led in the general direction they had chosen and they followed them. Fors was bending almost double under Arskane's weight when he caught a glimpse of something which brought hope and life back into him in one great surge. Only it was almost twilight and his eyes might have played him a trick—

No, he had been right! Those were tree tops ahead and

never had the sight of branches against an evening sky seemed so beautiful! Fors pulled Arskane's arm about his shoulders, dropped his bow, quiver and the Star pouch, and made that last dash.

After what seemed like days, weeks, later he lay face down in soft and natural earth, the good smell of leaf mold dank in his nostrils. And he heard the swish of rising wind through leaves which were true and green and clean. At last he raised his head. Arskane sprawled beyond. He had turned over on his back and his eyes were closed, but he was asleep. Fors sighed.

He must go back and recover the bow and the pouch before night closed in. But the struggle of getting to his feet made him grit his teeth. Odd—for the first time he noticed Lura was nowhere about. Hunting—maybe— But he must get that pouch! It was all the proof remaining that he had succeeded.

His feet dragged and his head was dizzy and queer. But he could keep to the line of footprints they had made and it was an easy guide back. He wavered on.

The walls of the first gully closed about him. When he glanced back he could see the trees but not where Arskane lay. It was growing darker—he must hurry.

A splitting pain broke in his head. He knew that he was falling and tried to throw out his hands to break that fall. But he only dimly felt the shock when he hit the ground. Instead he whirled out into a blackness which was complete.

First he was conscious of his body being jerked roughly, roughly enough to send pain shooting through it to the bursting agony in his head. Then he came out of the blackness, trying weakly to hold his thoughts together. The end to that first came when he fell again, struck painfully against solid rock and rolled. A kick in the ribs brought him to a racking stop. He must have been carried and thrown down. And the sickening stench in his nostrils told him by whom. He lay limply, not daring to open his eyes. As long as they deemed him senseless he might be safe for a while.

He was bound, his wrists behind the small of his back, his ankles together. Already his hands were numb and the bonds had cut his flesh. He could only listen and try to guess at what his captors were doing. They appeared to be settling down. He heard the grunt one gave, the scratching of nails across tough hide. Then, through rank body smell, he caught the scent of smoke and dared to peek beneath half-open lids.

Yes, they had kindled a fire, a fire which they were feeding with handfuls of a coarse grass they pulled up from where it grew along the sides of the valley. One came into the full light of the flames and flung down an armload of the water plants, still alive enough to attempt to writhe away from the heat.

But these were speedily seized upon and the red bulbs at their centers squeezed between yellowed fangs with snorts of satisfaction. Sucked dry, the plants were tossed on the fire. Fors swallowed with a bruised throat—his turn next?

But one of the Beast Things turned with inhuman swiftness and sprang to the wall behind it, clutching up something which wriggled and squeaked shrilly. It came back holding a squirming captive in each paw and batted the small bodies against a convenient rock until they were limp and still. The hunter's success aroused the envy of its fellows and they all pawed among the rocks of the valley, a few successfully.

Fors heard swift movement in the loose rocks somewhere behind him, as if small, agile things were speeding away to safety. The slowest of the hunters had returned to the fire grumbling and empty-handed. When the catch was laid out on the stone Fors saw it clearly for the first time—lizards! They resembled those he had seen all his life hiding among rocky places—and yet there was something odd about the shape of the heads— But before he could guess what it was the bodies had been slung over the flames to broil.

There were four Beast Things busy there. Either the whole clan had not after all ventured into the Blow-Up or else the party had split. But these four were bad enough. For the first time he was able to see them clearly.

They were probably no taller than he but their emaciated bodies perched on stick legs made them seem to top him. The grayish skin which was stretched tight over their sharp bones was deep grained, almost scaly, and their bodies were bare save for strips of filthy tattered stuff worn about their loins. But their faces—!

Fors forced himself to study, to study and file in memory what he saw. He tried to view those masks of horror with detachment. In general outline they were remotely human. But the eyes deep set in bone-rimmed pits, the elongated jaws above which the nose was only two slits—jaws equipped with a hunting beast's fangs—sharp fangs never fully covered by thin vestiges of lips—those were not human. They were—he recoiled from the picture formed in his mind—they were rats!

Fors shivered and could not control the trembling of his aching body. Then he tensed. Something was climbing down the slope behind him, not with the light patter of the lizards but with the assured tread of one who knows he has nothing to fear and is coming to meet friends. A moment later Fors felt a jar, then soft fur rolled against him. The steps went on.

Lura lay beside him now, her eyes wild with helpless rage, thongs about her paws, a loop holding her jaws tight together. Her tail beat across him. But when her eyes met Fors' she relaxed slightly. He could not move yet—

A fifth and sixth Beast Thing joined the others by the fire and were now demanding their share of the food. They were greeted with jeers until one growled some order and the meat was grudgingly shared. They ate in silence and when the leader was done it wiped its clawed fingers perfunctorily across its thighs before turning to examine some objects beside it.

Fors recognized his bow. The leader twanged the string curiously, hitting its thumb. With a savage growl it snapped the shaft between its fists and threw the broken weapon into the fire. The quiver followed, but the Beast Thing appreciated the worth of the steel arrowheads enough to break them off and put them aside.

When the creature took up the last piece of plunder—the Star pouch—Fors bit deep into his underlip. The precious contents were dumped out and went piece by piece into the flames. Map, journal, everything, except the small figures from the museum which seemed to fascinate the Beast Thing leader.

Having so examined the spoil the creature came over to the captives. Fors lay limp, willing each muscle to relax. Again a set of clawed toes, planted with breath-taking force in his short ribs, rolled him away from Lura and out into the full light of the fire. He struggled to keep under control his outrage and nausea as foul paws stripped from him every rag and fumbled over his body. What would come next, a knife, a blow strong enough to cave in his aching head? But strangely he was left while Lura underwent the same sort of inspection.

Then the claws twisted a hold in the thong which bound his wrists and he was pulled back to his former position, his back raked raw by the gravel. Lura was writhing violently. She had not relished her taste of the same treatment. Now she was tight against him, her thonged jaws pushed into his shoulder.

After a while Fors slept. When he roused again it was dim and gray with the false dawn. One of his captors hunched by the fire nodding, now and then feeding the flames. The rest lay curled in sodden sleep.

But Fors' mind was alert now. And he heard again very clearly the faint sounds made by the lizards passing among the rocks. Why should they venture back into a danger zone, he wondered. And then he saw what ringed the walls of the valley.

Terraces, hundreds of them, some only a few inches, some of them several feet wide, made a continuous stairway up the walls of the gulch. Each had been laboriously built up artificially, each was walled with pebbles and small stones. And on these tiny fields grew the grass stuff with which his captors fed their fire. They had stripped half the valley already. Even as he noticed the terraces for the first time the fire tender pulled an armload from its roots, denuding two more of the small fields.

Lizards and terraces—did the lizards make them? And those black holes showing at intervals along the topmost rim of the valley—what were they? He was answered by the sight of a scaled head—a sort of crest rising from its brow—which appeared in one as jewel bright eyes inspected the valley and the invaders.

Fors, now knowing what to look for, glanced around the rim of the valley. Heads! Heads popping in and out of the cave holes, appearing and disappearing with reptilian speed around stones and over the edges of the higher terraces. Always they moved almost without sound, so close to the rock in coloring and outline that only one who suspected them might even guess where and what they were.

If last night the lizards, surprised by a superior force, had fled, now they were back—with reinforcements. But at the best they stood only twenty inches high against the iron strength and greater bulk of the Beast Things who could crack their spines between thumb and forefinger. Why, an army would go down under the stamping feet of the enemy. But the lizards did not seem to be overawed by the odds against them.

Scouts advanced down the sides of the valley. From time to time Fors sighted slender shapes shooting from one piece of cover to another, always down toward the foe. Then he saw something else and could hardly believe his eyes. A party of lizards was issuing boldly out of one of the cave holes on the opposite side of the cut. They made no noise but neither did they make any effort to conceal their march. Instead they pattered down to the fields which the Beast Things had not yet torn up.

They walked on their hind legs in a curiously human stance and in the shorter front paws they each carried something. Down into their tiny meadows they paraded and set to work. Fors stared—they were reaping the grass, shearing off the blades and bundling them into shocks. And they worked without a single glance at what lay below, as if going about their business in the usual way.

Fors wanted to get up and shout a warning to those busy workers—for them to get away before the brutes by the fire sighted them. On the other hand, he was aware that an army, grim and intent upon some purpose, had gathered silently at the slope. Then he caught some glimmering of their plan and his head jerked up to see the better.

Bait! The lizards reaping up there were to be bait! Why, that was hard to believe. These—these little scaled creatures knew perfectly well what they were about—they were the heroes of the clan who had probably volunteered to man those terraces as bait. But even yet he did not realize to what extent the lizard folk would go to save their land.

The fire watcher yawned, belched, and stretched. Then it caught sight of the activity above. It grinned, its stained fangs widely displayed, and, reaching over, prodded one of the sleepers awake. At first the newly aroused one was inclined to resent it, but when the farmers above were pointed out to it, it rubbed the sleep from its eyes and proceeded to business.

From the gravel at its feet it picked out a handful of walnut-sized stones. And these both the Beast Things let fly with deadly accuracy. Two of the lizards kicked out their lives in the fields. The resulting shout of triumph from the hunters brought the whole camp awake.

But surely the lizards could take to cover quicker than they did! Fors watched with a queer sick feeling as one after another of the farmers failed to reach the safety of the cave holes. Then he understood—they had never intended to escape. They were giving their lives for the purpose of some plan they had made.

He would not watch the pitiful carnage any longer and he looked at the opposite side of the valley—just in time to see a small round object shoot out of the side of the hill and fall close to the camp fire. Another and another rattled down, as if brown hailstones were falling. Once they landed among the stones and loose gravel it was almost impossible to detect them. And if one had not rolled across a flat stone within touching distance he would never have known what they were.

A small ball, fashioned maybe of clay, was all he saw. But why were the small thorn points sticking out of its surface all the way around? If it was meant to wound, why shoot it while the Beast Things were all well away from the spot? Fors still puzzled over that as the victors came back swinging limp bodies and proud of their killing.

In spite of his revulsion Fors could not subdue the hunger pangs when the smell of the roasting meat was heavy on the air. He could only faintly remember his last meal—his stomach was one vast empty hollow. But neither did he want to attract the attention of those who were now wolfing down the half-cooked flesh.

One of the Beast Things, while reaching for another broiled lizard, gave a sudden exclamation and plucked something from its arm, hurling it away with the force of annoyance. It had been pricked by one of the lizard balls. But Fors could not see how that caused the victim any more than momentary discomfort. He watched closely and witnessed two of the creatures treading upon the thorn-studded globes. One of them did so when it went for a fresh supply of the water plants. And when it returned it walked slowly, stopping now and again to shake its narrow head and once to brush vigorously before its eyes as if to clear some obstruction hanging there.

They drank from the dying plants, sucked the last slender lizard bone clean, and got to their feet. Then they turned their attention to the captives. This was it! Fors grimaced. He had seen them impale and roast a screaming broken-legged lizard—

The Beast Things circled around the captives. There was a period of rough humor during which Fors was both kicked and slapped. But they were apparently not going to kill him now. Instead the leader stooped to slit the bonds about his ankles, the mountaineer's own knife in its paw.

That steel never bit into the hide. One of the brutes in the circle gave voice to a deep roar and bit at its own arm. Flecks of white foam showed in the corners of its jaws. It tore savagely at its own flesh and then started on an unsteady run down the valley. With grunts of astonishment the others remained where they were, watching their companion double up with a scream of anguish and fall into the fire.

Poison! Fors knew now the cleverness of the lizards, the reason for the sacrifice of the gleaners. The thorn balls were poisoned! And there had to be time for the poison to work. But—were they all infected?

In the end it was the leader who lived long enough to almost reach the other end of the valley, its paws scrabbling on the rock as it tried to drag its tortured body out of that place of death. But it crashed back, moaned twice, and then was as still as the rest.

Fors could hear the patter of lizard feet before he noticed that the hillsides were alive with them, moving in a red-brown cloud down toward the slain. He licked raw lips. Could he communicate with them, get them to use

that knife lying there to saw through his bonds? His
hands were numb and dead and so were his feet.

For a long time he hesitated as the lizards crowded
about the dead, their thin whistling echoing up and down
among the rocks. Then he ventured to make a croaking
sound which was all his dry throat and dryer mouth could
shape.

His answer was a flash of movement as those heads
snapped around and cold hard eyes regarded him with detachment. He tried again as Lura kicked for freedom to
no purpose. Some of the lizards drew together, their
crested heads bent as they conferred. Then a party started
forward. Fors tried to lift himself. Then sheer horror
caught at his nerves.

In each four-fingered paw they were carrying something—a branch thick with thorns!

11

✖ **Drums Speak Loudly**

"No! FRIEND—I AM FRIEND—" Fors gabbled the words wildly. But they were words the lizards did not recognize and the silent and menacing advance did not falter.

What stopped them was something else—a hissing from some point on the slope behind the helpless mountaineer. It was as if the giant grandfather of all snakes coiled there, resentful of the disturbance. To the lizards the hissing had meaning. They halted almost in midstep, their threadlike tongues flickering in and out, their ragged top crests stiff and upright, pulsing dark red.

Stones rattled down the hill. Fors tried desperately to turn his head to see what or who was coming. Lura's struggles increased in violence and he wondered if he could roll to that knife which lay just out of reach. Though his hands were dead and numb he might be able to saw through the cat's bonds.

One of the lizards drew ahead of the rest of the pack, but its thorn spear was still at "ready." The scaled throat swelled and an answering hiss sounded. That was replied

o promptly and afterward came three words which set
he captive's heart to pounding.

"Can you move?"

"No. And watch out! Poison thorns set in balls—on the
round—"

"I know." The answer was calm. "Keep still—"

Arskane hissed for the third time. The lizards drew
back, leaving their leader alone, alert and on guard. Then
Arskane was there, stooping to slash the bonds of both
captives. Fors tried to lever himself up with dead arms
which refused to obey him.

"Can—not—make—it—"

But Arskane was rubbing at the puffed and swollen
ankles and the torture of reviving circulation was almost
more than the mountaineer could bear without screaming.
t seemed only a second before Arskane hauled him to his
eet and pushed him toward the back slope.

"Get up there—"

That order had an urgency which made Fors climb in
pite of himself, Lura dragging up ahead. He dared not
waste the time to look back, he could only put all his
trength to the task of getting up to the top.

If the way had been steeper he might never have made
t. And as it was Arskane caught up to him and pulled
him along the last few steps. From the southerner's arm
ung Fors' knife belt with knife and sword both in their
sheaths—he had waited to retrieve that.

Neither of them lost time in talk, Fors glad to reel
along with the larger man's support. After a while he
knew that there was real grass under his feet and then he
slumped down where water sprayed his parched skin.

He did not know how much time passed before he
roused enough to know that Arskane was trying to pour
some broth down his throat. He swallowed eagerly until
his eyes closed against his will and he drifted off again.

"How did you get us out?" Fors lay at ease, hours
later. Under him a mat of ferns and leaves seemed almost

unbelievably soft and Arskane hunched on the other side of the fire fashioning a shaft for a short hunting spear.

"It was easy enough—with the Beast Things gone. I will tell you this with a straight and truthful tongue, brother." The southerner's teeth flashed white and amused in his dark face. "Had those yet breathed, then this venture might well have ended otherwise.

"When I awoke in this wood and found you gone I at first thought that you were hunting—for food or water or both. But I was not happy in my mind—not happy at all. I ate—here are rabbits, fat and foolish and without fear. And yonder there is the brook. So did my unease grow, for with food and drink so near I knew that you would not have gone from me and remained so long a time. So I went back along our trail—"

Fors studied the hands lumped on his chest, the hands which were still purplish and blue and which hurt with a nagging pain. What would have happened if Arskane had not gone back?

"That trail was very easy to follow. And along it I found the place where the Beast Things had lain in hiding to strike you down. They did nothing to cover their tracks. It is in my mind that they fear very little and see small need for caution. So came I at last to the valley of the lizards—"

"But how did you stop *their* attack?"

Arskane was examining a pile of stones he had culled out of the brook, weighing them in his hands and separating them into two piles. The smoothed spear shaft he had set aside.

"The lizard folk I have seen before. In my own land— or the land we held before the shaking of the mountains drove us forth—there was such a colony. They marched across the desert from the west one year and made a settlement in a gulch a half day's journey from the village of my people. We were curious about them and often watched them from a distance. At last we even traded—

giving them bits of metal in return for blue stones they grubbed out of the earth—our women having a liking for necklaces. I do not know what I said back there—I think it was only that my imitation of their speech surprised them so that they let us go.

"But it was well we got out of that place with all speed. The poison ball is their greatest weapon. I have seen them use it against coyote and snake. They wish only to be left alone."

"But—but they are almost—almost human—" Fors told of the gleaners and the sacrifice they had made for their clan.

Arskane laid out three stones of equal size and girth. "Can we then deny that they have a right to their valley? Could we show equal courage, I wonder?" He became busy with some thin strips of rabbit skin, weaving them into a net around each rock. Fors watched him, puzzled.

Just overhead there was a break in the mass of tree tops and as he lay back flat he could see the blue sky and part of a drifting white cloud. But this morning there was a chill tooth to the wind—summer was going. He must get back to the Eyrie soon—

Then he remembered what had happened to the Star pouch and his puffy fingers dug into the stuff he lay upon. There was no use in returning to the mountain hold now. When the Beast Things had destroyed his proof they had finished his chance of buying his way back into the clan. He had nothing left except what Arskane had brought out of the lizard valley for him—his knife and sword.

"Good!"

Fors was too sunk to turn his head and see what had brought that note of satisfaction into his companion's voice. Arskane did not have anything to worry about. He would go south and find his tribe, take his place among them again—

"Now we shall have food for the pot, brother—"

Fors frowned but he did look around. The southerner

stood there tall and straight and around his head he whirled a queer contraption that, to the mountaineer, seemed of no use at all. The three stones in their rabbit skin nets had been fastened to thongs of hide and the three thongs tied together with one central knot. This knot Arskane gripped between his fingers as he sent the stones skimming in a circle. Having tested it he laughed at Fors' bewilderment.

"We shall be moving south, brother, and in the level fields this will do very well, as I shall show you. Ha, and here now is dinner—"

Lura walked up to the fire carrying a young pig. She dropped her burden and with an almost human sigh plumped down beside the kill to watch Arskane butcher it skillfully.

Fors ate roasted pork and began to wonder if his lot was as hopeless as he had thought it to be. The Beast Things were dead. He might lie up until his full strength returned and then make a second visit to the city. Or if he did not dally there would still be time to reach the Eyrie and lead an expedition before winter closed in. He licked rich grease from his fingers and planned. Arskane sang the tune of mournful notes Fors had heard him hum at the fishing lake. Lura purred and washed her paws. It was all very peaceful.

"There faces us now," Arskane said suddenly, "the problem of clothes for you—"

"It faces me," Fors corrected him sleepily. "Unfortunately my wardrobe was left to amaze the lizards. And, strangely enough, I do not find in me any desire to reclaim it from them—"

Arskane tightened the knots on the ball and cord weapon. "There you may be wrong, my friend. A visit to the lizard valley—keeping to a safe distance, of course—might serve us very well."

Fors sat up. "How?"

"Five of the Beast Things died there. But how many followed us into the Blow-Up land?"

Fors tried to remember the size of the party he had spied upon. How large had it been? He could not truthfully say now, but he did have a disconcerting suspicion that there had been more than five in it. If that were so—why were they lingering here so close to the edge of the Blow-Up? His feet were good enough to enable him to put some miles between himself and the desolate waste which now lay only a half mile beyond them.

"Do you think that the lizards may have added to their bag?"

Arskane shrugged. "Now that they have been warned, perhaps they have. But we need the spoil they took. Your bow is gone, but those arrowheads would be useful—"

"Useful to the extent of daring the thorns?"

"Maybe." And Arskane fell to cross questioning him as to how much of his equipment the Beast Things had destroyed.

"Everything of value to me!" Fors' old feeling of helpless inadequacy closed in upon him. "They ripped the Star pouch to shreds and burned my notes and map—"

"There are the arrowheads," persisted Arskane. "Those were not burned."

Since he seemed to mean it when he urged such an expedition Fors began to believe that the southerner had some purpose of his own in mind. He himself saw no reason to return to the lizard valley. And he was still protesting within him when they came to the top of the rise down which Arskane had gone to the rescue. Lura had refused to accompany them any farther than the edge of the Blow-Up and they had left her there pacing back and forth, her flattened ears and moving tail emphatic arguments against such foolishness.

They stood looking down at a wild scene which almost turned Fors' stomach. He gulped and balled his puffed fingers into fists, so that the pain took his attention. The lizards might live upon the grass of the terraces but it appeared that they were also meat eaters and they were now making sure of the supply chance had brought them.

Two of the Beast Things were already but skeletons and the pack of the valley's inhabitants were fast at work on the others, a line of laden porters tramping up to the cave entrances while their fellows below swung tiny knives with the same skill with which the martyrs had earlier wielded their sickles.

"Look there—to the left of that rock—" Although Arskane's touch made pain shoot along the length of his arm Fors obediently looked.

There was a pile of stuff there. Fors identified the remnants of his leggings and a belt such as was worn by the Beast Things. But a glint of color just beyond the haphazard pile of loot was more interesting. It stood in a tiny hollow of the wall—three blue rods—just about a finger high—familiar—

Fors' puzzlement vanished. Those rods—they were the little figures he had brought from the museum in the Star pouch. Now they were set up—and before the feet of each was a pile of offerings!

They were gods. And with a sudden shock of illumination he knew why the lizard folk did them honor.

"Arskane! Those figures—there in that hollow—they are the ones I brought from the museum—and they are making offerings to them—worshiping them!"

The southerner rubbed his hand down his jaw in the familiar gesture which signified puzzlement. Then he fumbled in the traveling pouch at his own belt and brought out a fourth figure.

"They do it, don't you see—because of this!" Fors indicated the small head of the carving. Although the figure was human the head was that of a hook-billed bird of prey.

"One of those figures down there has the head of a lizard—or at least it looks like a lizard!"

"So. And thus—yes—I can see it!"

Arskane started down the slope and from his lips came the hissing cry he had used before. There was a flicker of movement. Fors blinked. The workers were gone, had melted into the cover of the rocks leaving the floor of the valley deserted.

The southerner waited, with a hunter's patience, one minute, two, before he hissed again. He was holding out between two fingers the bird-headed statue and its blue glaze was sharp and clear. Perhaps it was that which drew the lizard leaders from their cover.

They came warily, gliding around stones so that only the most intent watcher could sight them. And, Fors also saw with apprehension, they had their thorn spears with them. But Arskane was well above the line where those balls of clay had fallen. And now he put the blue figure down on the ground and retreated with long-legged strides uphill.

It was the statue which drew them. Three came together, flitting along with their peculiar scuttle. When they were within touching distance of the figure they stopped, their heads darting out at strange angles, as if to assure themselves that this was no trap-bait.

As one of them laid a paw upon the offering, Arskane moved, not toward them but in the direction of the pile of loot. He went cautiously, examining the ground by inches, paying no outward attention to the lizards. They stood frozen where they were, only their eyes following him.

Deliberately and methodically the southerner turned over what lay there. When he came back he carried Fors' boots and what was left of the mountaineer's clothing, passing the lizards as if they were not there. After he had passed by the leader grabbed the blue figure and darted away around a rock, his two fellows almost treading on his tail. Arskane came up slope with the same unhurried pace but there were beads of moisture across his forehead and cheeks.

Fors sat down and worked the boots over his sore feet. When he got up he looked once more into the valley. The workers were still skulking in their holes but there were now four instead of three blue figures standing in the rock shrine.

The next day they started south, leaving the queer Blow-Up land well behind them. And the second day they were deep in open fields where patches of self-sown grain rippled ripely under the sun.

Fors paused, half over a stone wall, to listen. The sound he had caught was too faint and low pitched for thunder, and it kept within the boundaries of a well-defined rhythm. "Wait!"

As Arskane stopped Fors realized where he had heard that before—it was the voice of a signal drum. And when he said so Arskane dropped down beside the stones, putting his ear to the ground. But the message ended too soon. The southerner got to his feet again, frowning.

"What—?" ventured Fors.

"That was the recall. Yes, you were right and it was a talking drum of my people and what it said is all bad. Evil comes now upon them and they must call back all spears to stand in defense of the clan—"

Arskane hesitated and Fors plunged.

"I am not a spearman, or now even a bowman. But still I wear a sword at my belt and I possess some skill in handling it. Shall we go?"

"How far?" he added another question some breathless minutes later. Arskane had taken him at his word and the steady lope which the southerner had set as their pace was easier matched by Lura's four feet than Fors' two.

"I can only guess. That drum was fashioned to summon across the desert country. Here it may be farther from us than it sounds."

Twice more that day they heard the summons rumble across the distant hills. It would continue to sound at intervals, Arskane said, until all the roving scouts returned.

That night the two sheltered in a grove of trees, but they did not light a fire. And before daylight they were on the trail once more.

Fors had not lost his sense of direction but this was new country, unknown to him from any account of the Star Men. The trip across the Blow-Up land had taken them so far off the territory on any map he had ever seen that he was entirely lost. He began to wonder privately if he could have returned to the Eyrie as he had so blithely planned, or made that trip without retracing his way through the city. This land was wide and the known trails very, very few.

On the third day they came to the river, the same one, Fors believed, he had crossed before. It was swollen with rain and they spent the better part of the day making a raft on which to cross. The current tore them off their course for several miles before they could make the leap ashore on the opposite side.

At sunset they heard the drum again and this time the throbbing was close to thunder. Arskane seemed to relax, he had had his proof that they were heading in the right direction. But as he listened to the continued roll, his hand went to the hilt of his knife.

"Danger!" He was reading the words out of the beat. "Danger—death—walks—danger—death—in—the —night—"

"It says that?"

He nodded. "The drum talk. But never before have I heard it speak those words. I tell you, brother, this is no common danger which sets our drums to such warnings. Listen!"

Arskane's upheld hand was not needed for Fors had caught the other sound before his companion had spoken. That light tap-tap was an answer, it was less carrying than the clan signal, but it was clear enough.

And again Arskane read the message: "Uran here— coming— That is Uran of the Swift Arm, the leader of our scouts. He ventured west as I came north at the faring forth. And—"

Once more the lighter sound of a scout's drum interrupted him.

"Balakan comes, Balakan comes. Now," Arskane moistened his lips, "there remains only Noraton who has not replied. Noraton—and I who cannot!"

But, though they waited tensely for long minutes, there was no other reply. Instead, after the period of silence, the clan signal broke again, to roll across the open fields, continuing so at intervals through the night.

They paused only to eat at dawn, keeping to the steady trot. But now the drum was silent and Fors thought that quiet ominous. He did not ask questions. Arskane's scowl was now permanent and he pressed on almost as if he had forgotten those who ran with him.

For smoother footing they took to one of the Old Ones' roads which went in the right direction and when it turned again moved into a game trail, splashing through a brook Lura took with a single bound. Deer flashed white tails and were gone. And now Fors saw something else. Black shapes wheeled across the sky. As he watched one broke away and drifted to earth. He caught at Arskane's swinging arm.

"The death birds!" He dragged the southerner to a stop. Where the death birds fed there was always trouble.

12

Where Sweep the Tides of War

WHAT THEY FOUND WAS A hollow pocket in the field and what lay therein on stained and trampled ground was not a pretty sight. Arskane went down on one knee by the limp body while Lura snarled and sprang at the foul birds that protested such interruption with loud screeching cries.

"Dead—a spear through him!"

"How long?" asked Fors.

"Maybe only this morning. Do you know this marking?" Arskane did some grisly work to hold up a broken shaft ending in a smeared leaf-shaped point.

"Plainsman made. And it is part of one of their lances, not a spear. But who—"

Arskane swabbed off the disfigured face of the dead with a handful of grass.

"Noraton!" The name was bitten off as his teeth snapped together. The other scout, the one who had not answered the summons.

Arskane wiped his hands, rubbing savagely as if he did

139

not want to think of what they had touched. His face was stone hard.

"When the tribe sends forth scouts, those scouts are sworn to certain things. To none were we to show an unsheathed sword unless they first attacked us. We would come in peace if we may. Noraton was a wise man and of cool, even temper. This was none of his provoking—"

"Your people are moving north to settle," mused Fors slowly. "The Plainspeople are proud-hearted and high of temper. They may see in your coming a threat to their way of life—they are much bound by custom and old ways—"

"So they would take to the sword to settle differences? Well, if that is as they wish—so be it!" Arskane straightened out the body.

Fors drew his sword, sawing through the turf. Together they worked in silence until they had ready a grave. And afterward, above that lonely resting place they piled up a mound to protect the sleeper. On its summit Arskane thrust deep the long knife Noraton had worn and the shadow of its cross hilt lay straight along the turned earth.

Now they pushed on through a haunted world. Death had struck Noraton down and that same death might now stand between them and the tribe. They held to cover, sacrificing speed once more to caution. Arskane took out his weapon of balls and thongs and carried it ready for action.

The end to their journey came as they skirted a small ruin and saw before them a wide stretch of open field. To use the cover afforded only at its far edge would mean a wide detour. Arskane chose to strike boldly across. Since the haste was his Fors accepted that decision, but he was glad that Lura scouted ahead.

Here the grass and wild grain was waist-high and a man could not run. It would entangle his feet and bring him down. Fors thought of snakes just as Arskane sprawled on his face, one foot in a hidden rabbit burrow.

He sat up quickly, his mouth working a little as he rubbed his ankle.

Fors' throat went tight. A clot of horsemen were pounding at them out of the shadow of the ruins, riding at a wild gallop, lance points forging a flashing wall before them.

The mountaineer flung himself on Arskane and they rolled just in time to escape being spitted by those iron tips, avoiding hoofs by so thin a hair of safety that Fors could hardly believe his skin intact. Arskane struggled out of his grasp as Fors got up, sword in hand. Just the proper weapon, he thought bleakly, with which to face armed horsemen.

Arskane whirled the ball weapon around his head and turned to meet the enemy. The force of their charge had taken them on too far to rein back quickly. But they had played this game before. They scattered out, fanning in a circle which would ring in their victims.

As they rode they laughed and made derisive gestures. That determined Fors. Short sword or no, he would take at least one of them down with him when the end came. The circling riders speeded their pace around and around, making their captives turn to face them at a dizzy rate.

But Lura spoiled that well-practiced maneuver. She reared out of the grass and swiped a paw full of raking claws down the smooth flank of a horse. With a terrible scream of fright and pain the animal reared and fought against the control of its rider. The horse won and raced out and away taking its rider with it.

Only—the rest were warned now and when Lura sprang again she not only missed but suffered the bite of an expertly aimed lance. However, her attacks gave Arskane the chance he had been waiting for. His ball weapon sang through the air and with uncanny precision wrapped itself about the throat of one of the lancers. He thudded limply into the tall grass.

Two—out of eight! And they could not run—even with

the circle broken. Such a move would lead only to Noraton's death with cold steel breaking from back to breast. The unharmed six had stopped laughing. Fors could guess what was being planned now. They would ride down the enemy, making very certain they should not escape.

Arskane balanced his long knife on the palm of his hand. The riders made a line, knee to knee. Fors jerked a hand to the left and the southerner's teeth showed in a mirthless smile. He pointed a finger right. They stood and waited. The charge came and they dared to watch a whole second before they moved.

Fors flung himself to the left and went down on one knee. He slashed up at the legs of the mount which came at him, slashed viciously with all his strength. Then he was up again with one hand twisted in the legging of the rider who stabbed down at him. He caught the blow on his sword and managed to hold on to the blade although his fingers went numb with the shock.

The rider catapulted into his arms and fingers dug into his cheeks just below his eyes sockets. There were tricks for close fighting, tricks which Langdon had passed to his son. Fors got on top and stayed there—or at least he did for a few victorious moments until he glimpsed a shadow sweeping in from the left. He dodged, but not quickly enough, and the blow sent him rolling free from the body of his opponent. He blinked painfully at the sky and was levering himself up on his elbows when a circle of hide rope dropped about his shoulders snapping his arms tight to his body.

So he sat dumbly in the grass. When he moved his ringing head too suddenly the world danced around in a sickening way.

"—this time no mistake, Vocar. We have taken two of the swine—the High Chief will be pleased—"

Fors picked the words out of the air. The slurring drawl of the Plainsmen's speech was strange but he had no difficulty in understanding it. He raised his head cautiously and looked around.

"—ham-strung White Bird! May night devils claw him into bits and hold high feast with him!"

A man came tramping away from a floundering horse. He walked straight to Fors and slapped him across the face with a methodical force and a very evident desire to hurt. Fors stared up at him and spat blood from torn lips. The fellow had a face easy to remember—that crooked scar across the chin was a brand not to be forgotten. And if fortune was at all good they would have a future reckoning for those blows.

"Loose my hands," Fors said, glad that his voice came out so steady and even. "Loose my hands, tall hero, and worse than night devils shall have your bones to pick!"

Another slap answered that, but before a second could be struck his assailant's wrist was caught and held.

"Tend your horse, Sati. This man was defending himself as best he knew. We are not Beast Things from the ruins to amuse ourselves with the tormenting of prisoners."

Fors forced his aching head up another inch so that he could see the speaker. The Plainsman was tall—he must almost top Arskane's height—but he was slighter and the hair tied back for riding was a warm chestnut brown. He was no green youth on his first war trail but a seasoned warrior. Lines of good humor bracketed his well-cut mouth.

"The other one is now awake, Vocar."

At that call the war chief turned his attention from Fors. "Bring him hither. We have a long trail to follow before sundown."

The floundering horse was stilled with an expert knife. But Sati arose from that task with the blackest of scowls for both captives.

Lura! Fors tried to glance across the grass without betraying interest or concern. The big cat had disappeared and since his captors did not mention her, surely she had not been killed. They would have been quick enough to claim her hide as a trophy. With Lura free and prepared to act there was a chance they might escape even yet. He held to that hope as they lashed his right hand fast to his own belt and fastened the left by a punishing loop to the saddle of one of the riders. Not to Sati's he was glad to note. That warrior had swung onto the horse of the man Arskane had killed with the ball loops.

And the southerner had taken other toll too. For there were two bodies lashed to nervous led horses. After some consultation two of the band went ahead on foot leading the burdened mounts. Fors' guard was the third in line of march and Vocar with Arskane at his side came near the end.

Fors looked back before the jerk at his wrist started him off. There was blood on the southerner's face and he walked stiffly, but he did not appear to be badly hurt. Where was Lura? He tried to send out a summoning thought and then closed his mind abruptly.

There had long been contact between the Eyrie and the Plainspeople. These men might well know of the big cats and their relationship with man. Best to leave well enough alone. He had no desire at all to watch Lura thrash out her life pinned to the hard earth by one of those murderous lances.

The line of march was westward, Fors noted mechanically, forced to keep a sort of loping run as the horse he was bound to cantered. The sun was hard and bright in their faces. He studied the paint marks of ownership dabbed on the smooth hide of the animal beside him. It was not a sign used by any tribe his people knew. And the speech of these men was larded with unfamiliar words. Another tribe on the move, maybe roving far distances. Perhaps, as Arskane's people, they had been driven out of their own grounds by some disaster of nature and were now seeking a new territory—or maybe they were only driven by the inborn restlessness of their kind.

If they were strange to this country their attitude of enmity against all comers was not so to be wondered at. Usually it was only the Beast Things who attacked without declaring formal war—without parley. If he only wore the Star—then he would have a talking point when he faced their high chief. The Star Men were known—known in far lands where they had never walked—and none had ever raised sword against them. Fors knew the bite of his old discontent. He was not a Star Man—he was nothing, a runaway and a wanderer who did not even dare claim tribe protection.

The dust pounded up by the hoofs powdered his face and body. He coughed, unable to shield his eyes or mouth. The horses went down a bank and splashed through a wide stream. On the other side they turned into a well-marked trail. A second party of riders issued out of the brush and shouted questions made the air ring.

Fors was a center of attention and the newcomers stared at him curiously. They discussed him with a frankness he tried to ignore and he held firmly to the rags of his temper.

He was not like the other one at all, was the gist of most of their comments. Apparently they already knew of Arskane's people and had little liking for them. But Fors, with his strange silver hair and lighter skin, was an unknown quantity which intrigued them.

The combined troops at last rode on, Fors thankful for the breathing spell he had been granted by the meeting. Within a half mile they came into their camp. Fors was amazed at the wide sweep of tent rows. This was no small family clan on the march, but a whole tribe or nation. He counted clan flags hung before sub-chieftains' tent homes as he was led down the wide road which divided the sprawling settlement into two parts. He had marked down ten and there were countless others to be seen fluttering back from this main path.

At the sight of the dead the women of the Plains city set up the shrill ritual wailing, but they made no move toward the prisoners who had been released from the saddle ties to have their hands lashed behind them and to be thrust into a small tent within the shadow of the High Chieftain's own circle.

Fors wriggled over on his side to face Arskane. Even in that dim light he could see that the southerner's right eye was almost swollen shut and that a shallow cut on his neck was closed with a paste of dust and dried blood.

"Do you know this tribe?" Arskane asked after two croaking attempts to shape the words with a dust-clogged tongue.

"No. Both the clan flags and their horse markings are new to me. And some of the words they use I have never heard before. I think that they have come a long way. The tribes the Star Men know do not attack without warning—except when they go against the Beast Things—for always are all men's swords bare to *them!* This is a nation on the march— I counted the banners of ten clans and I must have seen only a small portion of them."

"I would like to know what use they have for us," Arskane said dryly. "If they did not see profit in our capture we would now be awaiting the attention of the death birds. But why do they want us?"

Fors set himself to recall all that he had ever heard concerning the ways of the Plainspeople. They held freedom very high, refusing to be tied to any stretch of land lest it come to hold them. They did not lie—ever— that was part of their code. But also did they deem themselves greater than other men, and they had a haughty and abiding pride. They were inclined to be suspicious of new things and were much bound by custom—in spite of their talk of freedom. Among them a man's given word

was held unbreakable, he must always hold to a promise
no matter what might come. And anyone who offended
against the tribe was solemnly pronounced dead in
council. Thereafter no one could notice him and he could
claim neither food nor lodging—for the tribe he had
ceased to exist.

Star Men had lived in their tents. His own father had
taken a chief's daughter to wife. But that was only because the Star Men possessed something which the tribe
reckoned to be worth having—a knowledge of wide lands.

A wild burst of sound broke his thoughts, a sound
which grew louder, the full-throated chanting of fighting
men on the march.

> "With sword and flame before us,
> And the lances of clans at our backs,
> We ride through plains and forests
> Where sweep the tides of war!
> Eat, Death Birds, eat!
> From a feast we have spread for your tearing—"

A flute carried the refrain while a small drum beat out
the savage "eat, eat." It was a wild rhythm which made
the blood race through the listener's veins. Fors felt the
power of it and it was a heady wine. His own people were
a silent lot. The mountains must have drawn out of them
the desire for music, singing was left to the women who
sometimes hummed as they worked. He knew only the
council hymn which had a certain darksome power. The
men of the Eyrie never went singing into battle.

"These fighting men sing!" Arskane's whisper echoed
his own thoughts. "Do they welcome in such a manner
their high chief?"

But if it were the chief who was being so welcomed he
had no present interest in captives. Fors and Arskane remained imprisoned as the dreary hours passed. When it
was fully dark fires were lighted at regular intervals down
the main way and shortly after two men came in, to re-

lease them from the ropes and stand alert while they rubbed stiff hands. There were bowls of stew planked down before them. The stuff was well cooked and they were famished—they gave the food their full attention. But when he had licked the last drop from his lips Fors bent his tongue in the Plains language he had learned from his father.

"Ho—good riding to you, Plainsborn. Now, windrider, by the custom of the shelter fire and the water bowl, we would have speech with the high chief of this tribe—"

The guard's eyes widened. It was plain that the last thing he expected was to have the formal greeting of ceremony from this dirty and ragged prisoner. Recovering, he laughed and his companion joined jeeringly.

"Soon enough will you be brought before the High One, forest filth. And when you are that meeting will give you no pleasure!"

Again their hands were tied and they were left alone. Fors waited until he judged that their sentry was fully engaged in exchanging chaff with the two visitors. He wriggled close to Arskane.

"When they fed us they made a mistake. All Plainspeople have laws of hospitality. Should a stranger eat meat which has been cooked at their fires and drink water from their store, then they must hold him inviolate for a day, a night, and another day. They gave us stew to eat and in it was cooked meat and water. Keep silent when they lead us out and I shall claim protection under their own laws—"

Arskane's answering whisper was as faint. "They must believe us to be ignorant of their customs then—"

"Either that, or someone within this camp has given us a chance and waits now to see if we have wit enough to seize it. If that guard repeats my greeting then perhaps such an unknown will know that we are ready. Plainspeople visit much from tribe to tribe. There may be one or more here now who knows the Eyrie and would so give me a fighting change to save us."

Maybe it was that Fors' greeting had been passed on. At any rate, not many minutes elapsed before the men came back into the tent and the captives were pulled to their feet, to be herded between lines of armed men into the tall hide-walled pavilion which was the center of the city. Hundreds of deer and wild cattle had died to furnish the skins for that council room. And within it, packed so tightly that a sword could not lie comfortably between thigh and thigh, were the sub-chieftains, chiefs, warriors and wise men of the whole tribe.

Fors and Arskane were pushed down the open aisle which ran from the doorway to the center. There the ceremonial fire burned, sending out aromatic smoke as it was fed with bundles of dried herbs and lengths of cedar wood.

By the fire three men stood. The one, a long white cloak draped over his fighting garb, was the man of medicine, he who tended the bodies of the tribe. His companion who wore black was the Keeper of Records—the rememberer of past customs and law. Between them was the High Chief.

As the captives came forward Vocar arose out of the mass of his fellows and saluted the Chief with both hands to his forehead.

"Captain of Hosts, Leader of the Tribe of the Wind, feeder of the Death Birds, these two be those we took in fair fight when by your orders we scouted to the east. Now we of the clan of the Raging Bull do give them into your hands that you may do with them as you wish. I, Vocar, have spoken."

The High Chief acknowledged that with a brief nod. He was measuring the captives with a keen eye which missed nothing. Fors stared as boldly back.

He saw a man of early middle age, slender and wiry, marked with a strand of white hair which ran back across his head like a plumed crest. Old scars of many battle wounds showed under the heavy collar of ceremony which extended halfway down his chest. He was unmistakably a famous warrior.

But to be High Chief of a tribe he must be more than just a fighting man. He must also have the wit and ability to rule. Only a strong and equally wise hand could control a turbulent Plains city.

"You" —the Chief spoke first to Arskane— "are of those dark ones who now make war in the south—"

Arskane's one open eye met the Chief's without blinking.

"My people only go out upon the battlefield when war is forced upon them. Yesterday I found my tribesman food for the death birds and through his body there was a Plains lance—"

But the Chief did not answer that. He had already turned to Fors.

"And you—what tribe has spawned such as you?"

13

Ring of Fire

"I AM FORS OF THE PUMA CLAN, of the tribe of the Eyrie in the mountains which smoke." Because his hands were bound he did not give the salute of a free man to the commander of many tents. But neither did he hang his head nor show that he thought himself not the full equal of any in that company.

"Of this Eyrie I have never heard. And only far-riding scouts have ever seen the mountains which smoke. If you are not of the blood of the dark ones, why do you run with one of them?"

"We are battle comrades, he and I. Together we have fought the Beast Things and together we crossed the Blow-Up land—"

But at those words all three of the leaders before him looked incredulous and he of the white robe laughed, his mockery echoed a moment later by the High Chief, to be taken up by the whole company until the jeering roar was a thunder in the night.

"Now do we know that the tongue which lies within your jaws is a crooked one. For in the memory of men—

our fathers, and our fathers' fathers, and their fathers be-fore them, no men have crossed a Blow-Up land and lived to boast of it. Such territory is accursed and death comes horribly to those who venture into it. Speak true now, woodsrunner, or we shall deem you as twisted as a Beast One, fit only to cough out your life upon the point of a lance—and that speedily!"

Fors had clipped his rebel tongue between his teeth and so held it until the heat of his first anger died. When he had control of himself he answered steadily.

"Call me what you will, Chief. But, by whatever gods you own, will I swear that I speak the full truth. Perhaps in the years since our fathers' fathers' fathers went into the Blow-Up and perished, there has been a lessening of the evil blight—"

"You call yourself of the mountains," interrupted the White Robe. "I have heard of men from the mountains who venture forth into the empty lands to regain lost knowledge. These are sworn to the truth and speak no warped tales. If you be of their breed show us now the star which such wear upon them as the sign of their call-ing. Then shall we make you welcome under custom and law—"

"I am of the mountains," repeated Fors grimly. "But I am not a Star Man."

"Only outlaws and evil livers wander far from their clan brothers." It was the Black Robe who made that sug-gestion.

"And those are without protection of the law, meat for any man's ax. These men are not worth the trifling over—"

Now—now he must try his one and only argument. Fors looked straight at the Chief and interrupted him with the old, old formula his father had taught him years be-fore.

"By the flame, by the water, by the flesh, by the tent right, do we now claim refuge under the banner of this clan—we have eaten your meat and broken our thirsting here this hour!"

There was a sudden silence in the large tent. All the buzz of whispering from neighbor to neighbor was stilled and when one of the guards shifted his stance so that his sword hilt struck against another's the sound was like the call to battle.

The High Chief had thrust his thumbs between his wide belt and his middle and now he drummed on the leather with his finger tips, a tattoo of impatience. But the Black Robe moved forward a step reluctantly and gestured to the guard. So a knife flashed and the hide thongs fell from their cramped arms. Fors rubbed his wrists. He had won the first engagement but—

"From the hour of the lighting of the fires on this night until the proper hour you are guests." The Chief repeated those words as if they were bitter enough to twist his mouth. "Against custom we have no appeal. But be assured, when the time of grace is done, we shall have a reckoning with you—"

Fors dared now to smile. "We ask only for what is ours by the rights of your own custom, Chieftain and Captain of many tents." He made with his two hands the proper salute.

The High Chief's eyes were narrowed as he waved forward his two companions.

"And under custom these two be your guardians, strangers. You are in their care this night."

So they went forth from the council tent free in their persons, passing through the crowd to another hide-walled enclosure of smaller size. On the dark skins of which it was made various symbols were painted. Fors could make them out with the aid of the firelight. Some he knew well. The twin snakes coiled about a staff—that was the universal sign of the healer. And those balancing scales—those meant the equalizing of justice. The men of the Eyrie used both of those emblems too. The round ball with a flower of flames crowding out of its top was new but Arskane gave an exclamation of surprise as he stopped to point at a pair of outstretched wings supporting a pointed object between them.

"That—that is the sign of the Old Ones who were flying men. It is the chief sign of my own clan!"

And at those words of his the black-robed Plainsman turned quickly to demand with some fierceness:

"What know you of flying men, you creeper in the dirt?"

But Arskane was smiling proudly, his battered face alight, his head high.

"We of my tribe are sprung from flying men who came to rest in the deserts of the south after a great battle had struck most of their machines from the air and blasted from the earth the field from which they had flown. That is our sign." He touched almost lovingly the tip of the outstretched wing. "Around his neck now does Nath-al-sal, our High Chief, still wear such as that made of the Old One's shining metal, as it came from the hand of his father, and his father's father, and so back to the first and greatest of the flying men who came forth from the belly of the dead machine on the day they found refuge in our valley of the little river!"

As he talked the outrage faded from the Black Robe's face. He was a sadly puzzled man now.

"So does all knowledge come—in bits and patches," he said slowly. "Come within."

But it seemed to Fors that the law man of the Plainspeople had lost much of his hostility. And he even held aside the door flap with his own hands as if they were in truth honored guests instead of prisoners, reprieved but for a space.

Once inside they stared about them with frank curiosity. A long table made of polished boards set on stakes pounded into the earth ran down the center and on it in orderly piles were things Fors recognized from his few visits to the Star House. A stone hollowed for the grinding and bruising of herbs used in medicines, its pestle lying across it, together with rows of boxes and jars—that was the healer's property. And the dried bundles of twigs and leaves, hanging in ordered lines from the cord along the ridge pole, were his also.

But the books of parchment with protecting covers of thin wood, the ink horn and the pens laid ready, those were the tools of the law man. The records of the tribe were in his keeping, all the customs and history. Each book bore the sign of a clan carved on its cover, each was the storehouse of information about that family.

Arskane stabbed a finger at a piece of smoothed hide held taut in a wooden stretcher.

"The wide river?"

"Yes. You know of it, too?" The law man pushed aside a pile of books and brought the hide under the hanging lantern where oil-soaked tow burned to give light.

"This part—that is as I have seen it with my own two eyes." The southerner traced a curved line of blue paint which meandered across the sheet. "My tribe crossed right here. It took us four weeks to build the rafts. And two were swept away by the current so that we never saw those on them again. We lost twenty sheep in the flood as well. But here—my brother scouted north and he found another curve so—" Arskane corrected the line with his finger. "Also—when the mountains of our land poured out fire and shook the world around them the bitter sea waters came in here and here, and no more is it now land—only water—"

The law man frowned over his map. "So. Well, we have lived for ten tens of years along the great river and know this of its waters—many times it changes its bed and wanders to suit its will. There are the marks of the Old Ones' work at many places along it, they must have tried to hold it to its course. But that mystery we have lost—along with so much else—"

"If you have ridden from the banks of the great river you have come far," Fors observed. "What brought your tribe into these eastern lands?"

"Whatever takes the Plainspeople east or west? We have the wish to see new places born in us. North and south have we gone—from the edges of the great forests where the snows make a net to catch the feet of our horses and only the wild creatures may live fat in winter—to the swamp lands where scaled things hide in the rivers to pull down the unwary drinker—we have seen the land. Two seasons ago our High Chief died and his lance fell into the hand of Cantrul who has always been a seeker of far lands. So now do we walk new trails and open the world for the wonder of our children. Behold—"

He unhooked the lamp from its supporting cord and pulled Fors with him to the other end of the tent. There were maps, maps and pictures, pictures vivid enough to make the mountaineer gasp with wonder. They had in them the very magic with which the Old Ones had made their world live for one another.

"Here—this was made in the north—in winter when a man must walk with hide webs beneath his feet so that he sinks not into the snow to be swallowed as in quicksands. And here—look you—this is one of the forest people— they lay paint upon their faces and wear the hides of beasts upon their bodies but they walk in pride and say that they are a very ancient people who once owned all this land. And here and here—" He flipped over the framed parchment squares, the records of their travels set down in bright color.

"This—" Fors drew a deep breath— "this is greater treasure than the Star House holds. Could Jarl and the rest but look upon these!"

The law man ran his fingers along the smooth frame of the map he held.

"In all the tribe perhaps ten of our youth look upon these with any stir in their hearts or minds. The rest—

they care nothing for the records, for making a map of the way our feet have gone that day. To eat and to war, to ride and hunt, to raise a son after them to do likewise—that is the desire of the tribe. But always—always there are a few who still strive to go back along the old roads, to try to find again what was lost in the days of disaster. Bits and pieces we discover, a thread here and a tattered scrap there, and we try to weave it whole."

"If Marphy spoke now the full truth," the harsher voice of the healer broke in, "he would say that it was because he was born a seeker of knowledge that all this" —he waved at the array— "came to be. He it was who started making these and he trains those of like mind to see and set down what they have seen. All this has been done since he became keeper of the records."

The law man looked confused and then he smiled almost shyly. "Have I not said that it is in our blood to be ever hunting what lies beyond? In me it has taken this turn. In you, Fanyer, it also works so that you make your messes out of leaves and grass, and if you dared you would cut us open just to see what lies beneath our skins."

"Perhaps, perhaps. Dearly would I like to know what lies beneath the skins of these two that they have crossed the Blow-Up land and yet show no signs of the burning sickness—"

"I thought," retorted Arskane quickly, "that was the story you did not believe."

Fanyer considered him through narrowed eyes, almost, Fors thought, as if he did have the southerner opened for examination.

"So—maybe I do not believe it. But if it is true, then this is the greatest wonder I have yet heard of. Tell me, how did this thing happen?"

Arskane laughed. "Very well, we shall tell our tale. And we swear that it is a true one. But half of the tale belongs to each of us and so we tell it together."

And as the oil lamp sputtered overhead, guards and prisoners sat on the round cushions and talked and listened. When Fors spoke the last word Marphy stretched and shook himself as if he had been swimming in deep water.

"That is the truth, I think," he commented quietly. "And it is a brave story, fit to make a song for the singing about night fires."

"Tell me," Fanyer rounded abruptly upon Fors, "you who were lessoned for knowledge seeking, what was the thing which amazed you most in this journey of yours?"

Fors did not even have to consider his answer. "That the Beast Things are venturing forth from their dens into the open country. For, by all our observations, they have not done so before in the memory of men. And this may mean danger to come—"

Marphy looked to Fanyer and their eyes locked. Then the man of medical knowledge got to his feet and went purposefully out into the night. It was Arskane who broke the short silence with a question of his own.

"Recorder of the past, why did your young men hunt us down? Why do you march to war against my people? What has passed between our tribes that this is so?"

Marphy cleared his throat, almost as if he wished for time.

"Why? Why? Even the Old Ones never answered that. As you can see in the tumbled stones of their cities. Your people march north seeking a home, mine march east and south for the same reason. We are different in custom, in speech, in bearing. And man seems to fear this difference. Young blood is hot, there is a quarrel, a killing, from the spilled blood springs war. But chiefly the reason is this, I think. My people are rovers and they do not understand those who would build and root in one place within the borders of a land they call their own. Now we hear that a town is rising in the river bend one day's journey to the south. And that town is being settled by men of your blood. So now the tribe is uneasy and a little afraid of what they do not know. There are many among them who say that we must stamp out what may be a threat to us in time to come—"

Arskane wiped the palms of his hands across the tattered remnant of his garment, as if he had found those palms suddenly and betrayingly damp.

"In no way is my tribe any threat against the future of yours. We ask only for land in which to plant our seed and to provide grazing for our sheep. Perhaps we may be lucky to find a bank of clay to give us the material we need for our potters' craft. We are indifferent hunters—coming from a land where there is but little game. We have arts in our hands which might well serve others beside ourselves."

"True, true." Marphy nodded. "This desire for war with the stranger is our curse—perhaps the same one which was laid upon the Old Ones for their sins. But it will take greater than either of us to make a peace now—the war drums have sounded, the lances are ready—"

"And there, for once, you speak the full truth, oh, weaver of legends!"

It was the High Chief who came to the table. Laid aside were his feather helmet and cloak of office. In the guise of a simple warrior he could walk the camp unnoted.

"You forget this—a tribe which breeds not warriors to hold its lances will be swallowed up. The lion preys upon the bull—if it can escape the horns. The wolves run in packs to the kill. Kill or be killed, eat or be eaten—that is the law upheld better than all other laws."

Something hot rose in Fors' throat and he snapped out an answer to that which was born of this new emotion.

"The paws of the Beast Things are against all of us—in just that manner, oh Captain of the Tents. And they are no lightly considered enemy. Lead your lances against them—if war you must!"

Surprise came first into Cantrul's eyes and then the flush of anger stained his brown cheekbones. His hand moved instinctively to the hilt of his short sword. Fors' hands remained on his knees. The scabbard at his belt was empty and he could not accept any challenge the Plainsman might offer.

"Our lances move when they will and where they will, stranger. If they wish to clean out a nest of mud-hut-dwelling vermin—"

Arskane made no move, but his one unswollen eye calmly measured the High Chief with a control Fors admired. Cantrul wanted an answer—preferably a hot one. When it did not come he turned to Fors with a harsh question.

"You say that the Beast Things march?"

"No," Fors corrected him. "I say that for the first time in our knowledge they are coming fearlessly out of their burrows in the cities to roam the open lands. And they are cunning fighters with powers we have not yet fully gauged. They are not men as are we—even if their sires' sires' sires were of our breed. So they may be greater than we—or lesser. How can we yet know? But this is true—as we of the Eyrie, who have warred against them during generations of city looting, can say—they are enemies to mankind. My father died under their fangs. I, myself, have lain in their bonds. They are no common enemy to be dismissed without fear, Plainsman."

"There is this, remember." Marphy broke the short silence. "When these two fled across the Blow-Up land a pack of the creatures sniffed their trail. If we march south without taking care we may find ourselves with an enemy behind as well as before—to be caught between two fires—"

Cantrul's fingers drummed out a battle rhythm on his belt, a sharp furrow cut between his thin brows. "We have scouts out."

"True. You are a leader old in war knowledge. What is

needful has been ordered. Forgive me— I grow old, and conning records sometimes gives one a weary view of life. Man makes so many mistakes—sometimes it appears that never shall he learn—"

"In war he learns or dies! It is plain that the Old Ones did not or could not learn—well, they are gone, are they not? And we live—the tribe is strong. I think that you worry too much, both of you— Fanyer, too. We ride prepared and there is nothing that—"

But his words were drowned in such a thunder of sound that it seemed a storm had broken directly above the tent in which they stood. And through the general uproar came the shouts of men and the higher screaming of frightened women and children.

Those in the tent were across it in an instant, elbowing each other to be first at the door flap. The Plainsmen pushed out as Arskane pulled Fors back. As they hesitated they saw the wild stampede of horses pound down the center lane of the camp, threading around the fires with so little room that tents were going down under their hoofs. Behind, across the horizon, was a wavering wall of golden light.

Arskane's hand closed about Fors' wrist with almost bone-crushing pressure as he dragged the slighter mountaineer back into the tent.

"That is fire! Fire running through the prairie grass!" He had to shout the words in order to be heard over the tumult outside. "Our chance—"

But Fors had already grasped that. He broke out of the other's grip and ran down the length of the table looking for a weapon. A small spear was all he could see to snatch up. Arskane took the pestle of the herb grinder as Fors used the point of the spear to rip through the far wall of the tent.

Outside they headed away from the chieftain's enclosure, running and dodging among the tents, joining other running men in the shadows. In the stirred-up ant hill of the camp it was ridiculously easy to get away without notice. But the sky behind was growing steadily brighter and they knew they must get out of the camp quickly.

"It's sweeping around." Fors pointed out the swing of that ghastly parody of daylight. East and west the fire made a giant mouth open and ready to engulf the camp. There were fewer men running now and order was developing out of the first confusion.

They rounded the last of the tents and were out in the open, looking out for clumps of bushes or trees among which they could take cover. Then Fors caught a glimpse of something which brought him up short. A glare of yellow showed before them where it should not be—reflection—but how? A moment later Arskane verified his suspicion.

"It's a ring of fire!"

Fors' hunter's instincts began to work as those tongues of flame lapped skyward.

"Downhill!" He threw the order over his shoulder.

He could see a trampled trail marked by many hoofs, hoofs of horses led to water. Downhill was water!

Downhill they ran.

14

Arrow's Flight

THE WIND HAD CHANGED AND blinded by the smoke which
bit at eyes and throat they discovered the stream by
falling into it. In its depths they were not alone. A wave
of rabbits and other small furry things which squeaked
and scurried flooded out of the high grass to run along the
edge of the water, making small piteous sounds of fear
and terror until they plunged in to clog the water with
their bodies.

Out in midstream the smoke did not hang so thick.
Fors' night eyes adjusted and he took the lead, heading
down current, out toward where the flames bannered
high. The confused noise of the Plains camp died out as
the river turned a bend and a screen of willows closed in.

A deer crashed through the bushes, running, and behind it came a second and a third—then four more all together. The stream bed deepened. Fors' foot slipped off a
stone and his head went under. For a moment he knew
panic and then the art learned in mountain pools came
back to him and he swam steadily, Arskane splashing
along at his shoulder.

So they came out into the middle of a lake, a lake which ended in the straight line of a dam. Fors blinked water out of his eyes and saw round mounds rising above the stream line—beaver houses! He flinched as a big body floundered by to pull out its bulk on top of one of those lodges. A very wet and very angry wild cat crouched there, spitting at the liquid which had saved its life.

Fors trod water and looked back. Arskane's head was bobbing along as if the big man were in difficulties and the mountaineer turned back. Minutes later both clung to the rough side of the nearest lodge and Fors considered their future with cool calculation.

The beaver lake was of a good size and recent rains had added to its contents. Also the builders of the lodges and the dam had cleaned out the majority of the trees which had grown along its banks, leaving only brush. Seeing this the mountaineer relaxed. Luck had brought them to the one place which would save them. And he was not the only living thing to believe that.

An antlered buck swam in circles near them, its pronged head high. And smaller creatures were arriving by the dozens to clamber over each other up the sides of the lodges to safety. Arskane gave a violent exclamation of disgust and jerked back his hand as a snake wriggled across it.

As the fire crept along the shore, making the water as ruddy as blood, the creatures in the water and on the lodges seemed to cower, sniffing in the cindery hot breath of the flames reluctantly. A bird dropped out of the air, struck Fors' shoulder, and plumped into the water leaving a puff of burned feather stench behind it. The mountaineer dropped his head down on his hands, holding his mouth and nose only an inch or so above the water, feeling the blistering heat whip across his shoulders.

How long they remained there, their bodies floating in the water, their fingers dug into the stuff of the lodges, they never knew. But when the crackle of the fire diminished Fors raised his head again. The first of the blaze was gone. Here and there the stump of a tree still showed stubborn coals. It would be some time before they would dare walk over that still smoking ground. The water must continue to give them passage.

Fors fended off the body of a deer which had taken too late to refuge and worked his way to the next lodge and so on to the dam. Here the fire had eaten a hole, taken a good bite out, so that water was spilling freely into the old channel of the stream.

By the light of smoldering roots he could make out the course for some distance ahead.

"Holla!"

A moment later, Arskane joined him.

"So we follow the water, eh?" The southerner applauded. "Well, with the fire behind us we shall not worry about pursuit. Perhaps good fortune journeys on our right hand tonight, my brother."

Fors grunted, climbing over the rough surface of the dam. Again they could keep their feet. The water was only waist-deep here. But the stones in the course made slippery footing and they crept along fearing a disastrous fall.

When they were at last well away from the fire glow in the sky Fors stopped and studied the stars, looking for the familiar clusters which were the unchanging guides he had been taught. They were heading south—but from a westerly direction and this was unknown territory.

"Will we hear the drums now?" he asked.

"Do not count on it. The tribe probably believes me as dead as Noraton and sounds the call no longer."

Fors shivered, perhaps just from the long immersion in the chill water. "This is a wide land, without a guide we may miss them—"

"More likely to since this is war and my people will conceal what they may of the camp. But, brother, it is in my mind that we could not have won free so easily from this night's captivity had there not been a mission set upon us. Head south and let us hope that the same power will bring us to what we seek. At least your mountains will not move themselves from their root and we can turn to them if nothing better offers—"

But Fors refused to answer that, giving his attention again to the stars.

For the present they kept to the stream, stumbling between water-worn boulders and over gravel. At length they came into a ravine where walls of gray rock closed in as if they were entering the narrow throat of a trap. Here they pulled out on a flat ledge to rest.

Fors dozed uneasily. The mosquitoes settled and feasted in spite of his slaps. But at last his heavy head went flat and he could no longer fight off the deep sleep of a worn-out body and fatigue-dulled mind.

The murmur of water awoke him at last and he lay listening to it before he forced open puffy eyelids. He rubbed an itching, bite-swollen face as he focused dazedly upon moss-green rock and brown water. Then he sat up with a snap. It must be mid-morning at least!

Arskane still lay belly down beside him, his head pillowed on an arm. There was an angry red brand left by a burn on his shoulder—a drifting piece of wood must have struck there. And beyond Fors could see floating on the current other evidence of the fire—half-consumed sticks, the battered body of a squirrel with the fur charred from its back.

Fors retrieved that before the water bore it on. Half-burned squirrel was a rare banquet when a man's stomach was making a too intimate acquaintance with his backbone. He laid it out on the rock and worried off the skin with the point of the spear he had clung to through the night.

When he had completed that gory task he shook Arskane awake. The big man rolled over on his back with a sleepy protest, lay staring a moment into the sky, and then sat up. In the light of the day his battered face was almost a monster's mask mottled with purple brown. But he managed a lopsided grin as he reached for bits of half-raw meat Fors held out to him.

"Food—and a clear day for traveling ahead of us—"

"Half a day only," Fors corrected him, measuring the length of sun and shadow around them.

"Well, then, half a day—but a man can cover a good number of miles even in a half day. And it seems that we cannot be stopped, we two—"

Fors thought back over the wild activity of the past days. He had lost accurate count of time long since. There was no way of knowing how many days it had been since he had left the Eyrie. But there was a certain point of truth in what Arskane had just said—they had not yet been stopped—in spite of Beast Things, and Lizard folk, and the Plainsmen. Even fire or the Blow-Up land had not proved barriers—

"Do you remember what once I said to you, brother—back there when we stood on the field of the flying machines? Never again must man come to warfare with his own kind—for if he does, then shall man vanish utterly from the earth. The Old Ones began it with their wicked rain of death from the sky—if we continue—then are we lost and damned!"

"I remember."

"Now it lies in my mind," the big man continued slowly, "that we have been shown certain things, you and I, shown these things that we may in turn show others. These Plainsmen ride to war with my people—yet in them, too, is the thirst for the knowledge that the Old Ones in their stupid waste threw away. They breed seekers such as the man Marphy—with whom I find it in my heart to wish friendship. There is also you, who are mountain bred—yet you feel no hatred for me or for Marphy of the Plains. In all tribes we find men of good will—"

Fors licked his lips. "And if such men of good will could sit down together in common council—"

Arskane's battered face lit up. "My own thoughts spoken from your lips, brother! We must rid this land of war or we shall in the end eat each other up and what was begun long and long ago with the eggs of death laid by our fathers from the sky shall end in swords and spears running sticky red—leaving the land to the Beast Things. And that foulness I shall not believe!"

"Cantrul said that his people must fight or die—"

"So? Well, there are different kinds of warfare. In the desert my people fought each day, but their enemies were sand and heat, the barren land itself. And if we had not lost the ancient learning perhaps we might even have tamed the burning mountains! Yes, man must fight or he becomes a soft nothing—but let him fight to build instead of to destroy. I would see my people trading wares and learning with those born in tents, sitting at council fires with the men of the mountain clans. Now is the time we must act to save that dream. For if the people of the tents march south in war they shall light such a fire as we or no living man may put out again. And in that fire we shall be as the trees and grass of the fields—utterly consumed."

Fors' answer was a grim stretch of ash-powdered skin which in no way resembled a smile. "We be but two, Arskane, and doubtless I am proclaimed outlaw, if the men of the Eyrie have noted my flight at all. My chance of gaining a hearing of their councils was destroyed by the Beast Things when they burned my city records. And you—?"

"There is thus much, brother. I am a son of a Wearer of the Wings—though I am youngest and least of the family clan. So perhaps some will listen to me, if only for a space. But we must reach the tribe before the Plainsmen do."

Fors tossed a cleaned bone into the water below.

"Heigh-ho! Then it is foot slogging again. I wish that we might have brought one of those high-stepping pacers out of the herds. Four legs are better than two when there is speed to consider."

"Afoot we go." But Arskane could not suppress an exclamation of pain as he got to his feet and Fors could see that he favored the side where the shoulder wound still showed red. However, neither made any complaint as they jumped down from the ledge and plodded on through the ravine.

Arskane was dreaming a dream and it was a great dream, Fors thought, almost with a prick of real envy. He himself drew bow cord against the Beast Things without any squeamishness, and he could fight with everything in him when his life was at stake as it had been when they were cornered by the Plainsmen. But he took no joy in slaying—he never had. As a hunter he had killed only to fill his belly or for the pots of the Eyrie. He did not like the idea of notching an arrow against Marphy or of standing against Vocar with bare swords—for no good reason save a lust to battle—

Why had the men of the Eyrie drawn apart from their kind all these years? Oh, he knew the old legends—that they were sprung from chosen men who with their womenkind had been hidden in the mountains to escape just such an end as tore their civilization into bloody shreds. They had been sent there to treasure their learning—so they did, and tried to win more.

But had they not also come to believe themselves a superior race? If his father had not broken the unwritten law and married with a stranger, if he himself had been born of pure clan blood within the walls of the Eyrie—would he think now as he did? Jarl—his father had liked Jarl, had held him in high respect, had been the first to give him the salute when he had been raised to the Captaincy of the Star Men. Jarl!—Jarl could speak with Marphy and they would be two quick minds talking—

hungrily. But Jarl and Cantrul—no. Cantrul was of a different breed. Yet he was a man whom others would follow always—their eyes on that head, held high, with its startling plume of white hair—a battle standard.

He himself was a mutant, a thing of mixed strains. Could he dare to speak for anyone save himself? At any rate he knew what he wanted now—to follow Arskane's dream. He might not believe that that dream would ever come true. But the fight for it would be his battle. He had wanted a star for his own—the silver star which he could hold in his two hands and wear as a badge of honor to compel respect from the people who had rejected him. But Arskane was showing him now something which might be greater than any star. Wait—wait and see.

His feet fell easily into the rhythm of those two words. The stream curved suddenly when it issued out of the ravine. Arskane pulled himself up the steep bank by the help of bushes. Fors gained the top in the same moment and together they saw what lay to the south. A dense column of smoke mushroomed into the sky of later afternoon.

For one startled minute Fors thought of the prairie fire. But surely that had not spread here, they had passed the line of burning hours back. Another fire, and a localized one by the line of smoke. One could take a route leading along the row of trees to the right, snake through the field of tangled bushes beyond where red fruit hung heavy and ripe, and reach the source without being exposed to attack.

Fors felt the rake of berry thorns on his flesh, but at the same time he crammed the tartly sweet fruit into his mouth as he crawled, staining his hands and face with dark juice.

Halfway across the berry patch they came upon evidence of a struggle. Under a bush lay a tightly woven basket, spilling berries out into a mush of trampled earth and crushed fruit. From this a trail of beaten-down grass and broken bushes led to the other side of the field.

From the tight grasp of briars Arskane detached a strip of cloth dyed a dull orange. He pulled it slowly through his fingers.

"This is of my tribal making," he said. "They were berrying here when—"

Fors felt the point of the spear he trailed. It was not much of a weapon. He longed fiercely for his bow—or even to hold the sword the Plainsmen had taken from him. There were sword tricks which could serve a man well at the right occasion.

With the scrap of cotton caught between his teeth Arskane crawled on, giving no heed to the thorns which ripped his arms and shoulders. Fors was conscious now of a thin wailing sound, which did not rise or fall but kept querulously to one ear-torturing note. It seemed to come with the smoke which the wind bore to them.

The berry field ended in a stand of trees and through these they looked out upon a lost battlefield. Small, two-wheeled carts had been pulled up in a circle, or into a segment of a circle, for there was a large gap in it now. And on these carts perched death birds, too stuffed to do more than hold on to the wood and stare down at a feast still spread to entice them. A mound of gray-white bodies lay at one side, the thick wool on them clotted and stiffened with blood.

Arskane got to his feet—where the birds roosted unafraid the enemy was long gone. That monotonous crying still filled the ears and Fors began to search for the source. Arskane stooped suddenly and struck with a stone grabbed from the ground. The cry was stilled and Fors saw his companion straighten up from the still quivering body of a lamb.

There was another quest before them, a more ghastly one. They began it with tight mouths and sick eyes— dreading to find what must lie among the burning wagons and the mounds of dead animals. But it was Fors who found there the first trace of the enemy.

He half stumbled over a broken wagon wheel and beneath it was a lean body which lay with arms outstretched and sightless eyes staring up. From the hairless chest protruded the butt of an arrow which had gone true to its mark. And that arrow—! Fors touched the delicately set features at the end of the shaft. He knew the workmanship—he himself set feathers in much the same fashion. Though here was no personal mark of ownership—nothing but the tiny silver star set so deeply into that shaft that it could never be effaced.

"Beast Thing!" Arskane exclaimed at the sight of the corpse.

But Fors pointed to the arrow. "That came from the quiver of a Star Man."

Arskane did not display much interest—there were his own discoveries.

"This is the encampment of a family clan only. Four wagons are burning, at least five escaped. They could not run with the sheep—so they killed the flock. I have found the bodies of four more of these vermin—" He touched the Beast Thing with the toe of his moccasin.

Fors stepped across the hind legs of a dead pony which still lay with the harness of a cart on it. A Beast Thing dart stood out between its ribs. From the presence of the Beast Thing corpses, Fors was inclined to believe that the attack had been beaten off and the besieged had been successful in the break for freedom.

A second search of the litter equipped them with darts, and Fors snapped off the shaft of the arrow which bore the star marking. Some wanderer from the Eyrie had made common cause with the southerners in this attack. Did that mean that he could expect to meet a friend—or an enemy—when he joined Arskane's people?

The wheels of the escaping carts had cut deep ruts in the soft turf and there were footprints clear to read beside them. The death birds settled back to the feast as the two moved on. Arskane was breathing hard and the grimness which had cut his mouth into a cruel line over the grave of Noraton was back.

"Four of the Beast Things," puzzled Fors, lengthening his stride to a lope to keep up. "And the Lizard folk killed five. How many are out roving— There has never been such an onslaught of the things before. Why—?"

"I found a burned-out torch in the paw of one of them back there. Maybe the fire of the Plains camp came from their setting. Just as they tried here to fire the carts and drive out the clan to slaughter."

"But never before have they come out of the ruins. Why now?"

Arskane's lips moved as if he would spit. "Perhaps they too seek land—or war—or merely the death of all those not of their breed. How can we look into the minds of such? Ha!"

The cart track they followed joined another—a deeper, wider track, such a road as must have been beaten down by the feet and wheels of a nation on the march. The tribe was ahead now.

In the next second, Fors checked so suddenly that he came near to tripping over his own feet. Out of nowhere had come an arrow, to dig deep into the earth and stand, quivering a little, an arrogant warning and a threat. He did not have to examine it closely. He knew before he put out his hand that he would find a star printed in its shaft.

15

Bait

ARSKANE DID NOT BREAK STRIDE but threw himself to the left and crouched in the shadow of a bush, the darts he had picked up at the scene of the ambush in his hands, ready. Fors on the contrary stood where he was and held up empty palms.

"We travel in peace—"

The rolling words of his own mountain land seemed odd to mouth after all these weeks. But he was not surprised at the identity of the man who came out of the clump of trees to the right of the trail.

Jarl would be imposing even in the simple garb of one of the least of the Eyrie. In the insignia of the Star Captain he had more majesty, thought Fors proudly, than Cantrul, for all the Plainschief's feather helmet and collar of ceremony. As he walked toward them the sun glinted meteor bright on the Star at his throat and on the well-polished metal of belt, sword hilt and knife guard.

Arskane pulled his feet under him. He was like Lura ready to spring for the kill. Fors made a furious gesture at him. Jarl, in turn, showed no astonishment at the sight of the two who waited for him.

"So, kinsman." He fingered his bow as if it were a councilor's staff of office. "This is the trail you have found to follow?"

Fors saluted him. And when Jarl did not acknowledge that courtesy he bit down hard on the soft inner part of his lip. True, Jarl had never shown him any favor in the past, but neither had the Star Captain ever by word or deed betrayed belief that Fors was any different from the rest of the young of the Eyrie. And for that he had long ago won a place apart in the boy's feelings.

"I travel with Arskane of the Dark Ones, my brother." He snapped his fingers to bring the southerner out of the bush. "His people are in danger now, so we join them—"

"You realize that you are now outlawed?"

Fors tasted the flat sweetness of the blood from his lip. He could, in all fairness, have hoped for little less than that sentence after his manner of leaving the Eyrie. Nevertheless the calm mention of it now made him cringe a little. He hoped that he did not show his discomfiture to Jarl. The Eyrie had not been a happy home for him—he had never been welcome there since Langdon's death. In truth they had outlawed him long since. But it had been the only shelter he knew.

"By the fire of Arskane is his brother always welcome!"

Jarl's eyes, those eyes which held one on the balance scale, went from Fors to his companion.

"Soon the Dark Ones will not have fires or shelter to offer. You are late in your returning, clansman. The drums of recall have been still these many hours."

"We were detained against our will," returned Arskane almost absently. He was studying Jarl in his turn and, seemingly, the result was not altogether to his liking.

"And not detained in gentleness it would appear." Jarl must have marked every cut and bruise the two before him boasted. "Well, fighting men were always welcome before a battle."

"Have the Plainsmen—?" began Fors, truly startled. That Cantrul could have moved so quickly out of the wild confusion they had left him in was almost beyond belief.

"Plainsmen?" He had shaken Jarl. "There are no Plainsmen in this. The Beast Things have forsaken their ways and are boiling out of their dens. Now they move in numbers to make war against all humankind!"

Arskane put his hand to his head. He was tired to exhaustion, his lips showing white under the swelling which made a lopsided lump of half his mouth. Without another word he started on doggedly but when Fors would have followed him the Star Captain put out a hand which brought him up short.

"What is this babble of Plainsmen attacking—?"

Fors found himself answering with the story of their capture and stay in the Plains camp and their escape from Cantrul's tent city. By the time he had finished Arskane was already out of sight. But still Jarl made no move to let him go. Instead he was studying the patterns he traced in the dust with the tip of his long bow. Fors impatiently shifted weight from one foot to the other. But when the Star Captain spoke it was as if he followed his own thoughts.

"Now do I better understand the events of these past two days."

He whistled high and shrill between his teeth, the sound carrying far as Fors knew.

And he was answered when out of the grass came two lithe furry bodies. Fors did not notice the black one that rubbed against Jarl—for he was rolling across the ground where the force of the other's welcome had sent him, rolling and laughing a little hysterically as Lura's rough tongue explored his face and her paws knocked him about with heavy tenderness.

"Yesterday Nag came back from hunting and brought

her with him." Jarl's hand rubbed with steady strokes behind the ears of the huge cat whose black fur, long and silky and almost blue in the sun, twisted in his fingers. "There is a lump on her skull. During your fight she must have been knocked unconscious. And ever since Nag brought her in she has been trying to urge me into some task—doubtless the singlehanded rescue of your person—"

Fors got to his feet while Lura wove about him, butting at him with her head and rubbing against his none too steady legs with the full force of her steel-tendoned body.

"Touching sight—"

Fors winced. He knew that tone from Jarl. It had the ability to deflate the most confident man and that speedily. With an unspoken suggestion to Lura he started down the trail after the vanished Arskane. Although he did not look back he knew that the Star Captain was following him at the easy, mile-eating pace his own feet had automatically dropped into.

Jarl did not speak again, remaining as silent as Nag, that black shadow which slipped across the land as if he were only in truth the projection of a bush in the sun. And Lura, purring loudly, kept close to Fors' side as if she were afraid that should she return to her old outflanking ways he would disappear again.

They found Arskane's people encamped in a meadow which was encircled on three sides by a river. The two-wheeled carts were a wooden wall around the outer edges and in the center showed the gray backs of sheep, the dun coats of ponies in rope corrals with the lines of family cooking fires running between low tents. There were only a few men there and those were fully armed. Fors suspected that he must have come through some picket line unchallenged because of the Star Captain's companionship.

It was easy to find Arskane. A group of men and a large circle of women ringed him. It was a crowd so intent upon the scout's report that not one of them noted the arrival of Fors and Jarl.

Arskane was talking to a woman. She was almost as tall as the young warrior before her and her features were strongly marked. Two long braids of black hair swung down upon her shoulders and now and again she raised a hand to push at them impatiently with a gesture which had become habitual. Her long robe was dyed the same odd shade of dusky orange as the scrap of cotton they had found in the berry field and on her arms and about her neck was the gleam of stone-set silver.

As Arskane finished, she considered for a moment and then a stream of commands, spoken too rapidly in the slurred tongue of the south for Fors to follow, sent the circle about her apart, men and women both hurrying off on errands. When the last of these left she caught sight of Fors and her eyes widened. Arskane turned to see what had surprised her. Then his hand fell on the mountaineer's shoulder and he pulled him forward.

"This is he of whom I have told you—he has saved my life in the City of the Beast Things, and I have named him brother—"

There was almost a touch of pleading in his voice.

"We be the Dark People." The woman's tone was low but there was a lilt in it, almost as if she chanted. "We be the Dark People, my son. He is not of our breed—"

Arskane's hands went out in a nervous gesture. "He is my brother," he repeated stubbornly. "Were it not for him I would have long since died the death and my clan would never have known how or where that chanced."

"In turn," Fors spoke to this woman chief as equal to equal, "Arskane has stood between me and a worse passing—has he neglected to tell you that? But, Lady, you should know this— I am outlawed and so free meat to any man's spear—"

"So? Well, the matter of outlawry is between you and

your name clan—and not for the fingering of strangers. You have a white skin—but in the hour of danger what matters the color of a fighting man's bone covering? The hour is coming when we shall need every bender of bow and wielder of sword we can lay orders upon." She stooped and caught up a pinch of the sandy loam which ridged between her sandaled feet. And now she stretched out her hand palm up with that bit of earth lying on it.

Fors touched the tip of his forefinger to his lips and then to the soil. But he did not fall to his knees in the finish of that ritual. He gave allegiance but he did not beg entrance to a clan. The woman nodded approvingly.

"You think straight thoughts, young man. In the name of the Silver Wings and of Those Who Once Flew, I accept your fighting faith until the hour when we mutually agree to go our ways. Now are you satisfied, Arskane?"

Her clansman hesitated before he answered. There was an odd soberness on his face as he regarded Fors. Plainly he was disappointed at the mountaineer's refusal to ask for clan standing. But at last he said:

"I claim him as a member of my family clan, to fight under our banner and eat at our fire—"

"So be it." She dismissed them both with a wave of her hand. Already she looked beyond them to Jarl and was summoning the Star Captain imperiously.

Arskane threaded through the camp, giving only hasty greetings to those who would have stopped him, until he came to a tent which had two carts for walls and a wide sweep of woolen stuff for a roof. Round shields of rough-scaled skin hung in a row on mounts by the entrance— four of them—and above these warrior shields the wind played with a small banner. For the second time Fors saw the pattern of the widespread wings, and below those a scarlet shooting star.

A small, grave-eyed girl glanced up as they came. With a little cry she dropped the pottery jar she had been holding and came running, to cling tightly to Arskane, her face hidden against his scarred body. He gave a choked laugh and swept her up high.

"This is the small-small one of our hearthside, my brother. She is named Rosann of the Bright Eyes. Ha, small one, bid welcome my brother—"

Shy dark eyes peered at Fors and then little hands swept back braids which would in a few years rival those of the woman chief and an imperious voice ordered Arskane to "put me down!" Once on her two feet again she came up to the mountaineer, her hands outstretched. Half guessing the right response Fors held out his in turn and she laid small palms to press his large ones.

"To the fire on the hearth, to the roof against the night and storm, to the food and drink within this house, are you truly welcome, brother of my brother." She said the last word in triumph at her perfect memory and smiled back at Arskane with no little pride.

"Well done, little sister. You are the proper lady of this clan house—"

"I accept of your welcome, Lady Rosann." Fors showed more courtliness than had been in his manner when he had greeted the chieftainess.

"Now," Arskane was frowning again, "I must go to my father, Fors. He is making the rounds of the outposts. If you will await us here—"

Rosann had kept hold of his hand and now she gave him the same wild smile with which she had favored her brother. "There are berries, brother of my brother, and the new cheese and corn cake fresh baked—"

"A feast—!" He met her smile.

"A true feast! Because Arskane has come back. Becie said that he would not and she cried—"

"Did she?" There was an unusual amount of interest in that comment from her tall brother. Then he was gone, striding away between the tent lines. Rosann nodded.

"Yes, Becie cried. But I did not. Because I knew that he would be back—"

"And why were you so sure?"

The hand tugged him closer to the shield stands. "Arskane is a great warrior. That—" a pink-brown finger touched the rim of the last shield in the row, "that is made from the skin of a thunder lizard and Arskane killed it all alone, just himself. Even my father allowed the legend singer to put together words for that at the next singing time—though he has many times said that the son of a chief must not be honored above other warriors. Arskane—he is very strong—"

And Fors, remembering the days just past, agreed. "He is strong and a mighty warrior and he has done other things your legend singer must weave words about."

"You are not of our people. Your skin" —she compared his hand with hers— "it is light. And your hair—it is like Becie's necklace when the sun shines upon it. You are not of us Dark People—"

Fors shook his head. In that company of warm brown skins and black hair his own lighter hide and silver headcapping must be doubly conspicuous.

"I come from the mountains—far to the east—" He waved a hand.

"Then you must be of the cat people!"

Fors' gaze followed her pointing finger. Nag and Lura sat together at a good distance from the sheep and the tough little ponies as they had apparently been ordered to do. But, at Fors' welcoming thought, Lura came up, leaving Nag behind. Rosann laughed with pure delight and threw her arms around the cat's neck, hugging her tight. The rumble of Lura's purr was her answer and a rough pink tongue caressed her wrist.

"Do all you people of the mountains have the big cats for your own friends?"

"Not all. The cat ones are not so many and it is for

them to choose with whom they will hunt. This is Lura who is my good friend and roving companion. And that yonder is Nag who runs with the Star Captain."

"I know—the Star Captain Jarl, he who has the kind eyes. He talks in the night with my father."

"Kind eyes." Fors was a little startled at a description so at variance with what he thought he knew. Though Rosann probably did not see Jarl as he appeared to a mutant and tribal outlaw.

Smoke was rising from the line of fires and borne with it was the fragrance of cooking. Fors could not repress a single sniff.

"You are hungry, brother of my brother!"

"Maybe—just a little—"

Rosann flushed. "I am sorry. Again have I let my tongue run and not remembered the Three Duties. Truly am I shamed—"

Her fingers tightened on his and she pulled him under the entrance flap of the tent.

"Down!"

Fors' heels struck against a pile of thick mats and he obediently folded up his long legs and sat. Lura collapsed beside him as Rosann bustled about. Before Fors could even make out the patterns of the hangings on the walls Rosann returned, carrying before her a wide metal basin of water from which rose steam and the spicy scent of herbs. A towel of coarse stuff lay over her arm and she held it ready as Fors washed.

Then came a tray with a spoon and bowl and a small cup of the same bitter drink he had brewed under Arskane's direction in the museum. The corn mush had been cooked with bits of rich meat and the stimulating drink was comforting in his middle.

He must have dozed off afterward because when he roused it was night outside and the crimson flames of the fire and the lesser beams of a lamp fought against the shadows. A hand placed on his forehead had brought him awake. Arskane knelt beside him and there were two others beyond. Fors levered himself up.

"What—" He was still half asleep.

"My father wishes to speak with you—"

Fors gathered his wits. One of the men facing him now was a slightly older edition of his friend. But the other wore about his throat a pair of silver wings fastened to a chain of the same stuff.

The chieftain was smaller than his sons and his dark skin was seamed and cracked by torrid winds and blistering suns. Across his chin was the ragged scar of an old and badly healed wound. Now and again he rubbed at this with a forefinger as if it still troubled him.

"You are Fors of the mountain clans?"

Fors hesitated. "I was of those clans. But now I am outlaw—"

"The Lady Nephata gave him earth—"

Arskane was both interrupted and effectively silenced by a single sharp look from his father.

"My son has told us something of your wanderings. But I would hear more of this Plainsmen encampment and what chanced with you there—"

For the second time Fors repeated his outline of recent events. When he had finished the Chief favored him with the same sort of intimidating glare which had worked on his son a few minutes before. But Fors met it forthrightly.

"You, Rance," the Chief turned to the young man with him, "will alert the scouts against this trouble and make the rounds of the western outposts every hour. If an attack offers, the two beacons on the round hills must be fired. That you must keep ever in the minds of the men—"

"You see, rover" —the Chief spoke over his shoulder, addressing a shadow near the door, and for the first time Fors noted a fourth man there— "we do not go to war as to a banquet—as these Plainsmen seem to do. But if it be necessary then we can fight! We who have faced the wrath of the thunder lizards and taken their hides to make our shields of ceremony—"

"Do not greatly fear the lances of mere men." The Star Captain appeared faintly amused. "Perhaps you are right, Lanard. But do not forget that the Beast Things are also abroad and they are less than men—or more!"

"Since I have ordered the war drums for more than the lifetime of this my youngest son, I do not forget one danger when faced by another, stranger!"

"Your pardon, Lanard. Only a fool tries to teach the otter to swim. Let war be left to the warriors—"

"Warriors who have sat too long at their ease!" snapped the chieftain. "To your posts, all of you!"

Arskane and his brother went, the chieftain stamping out impatiently after them. Fors started to follow.

"Wait!"

There was the crack of a whip in that one word. Fors stiffened. Jarl had no power of command over him—not even the faintest shadow of power if he was an outlaw. But he dropped his hand on Lura's head and waited.

"These people," Jarl continued with the same harsh abruptness, "may be broken between two enemies. It is not in their nature to back trail and in their own country there has been nothing they could not vanquish. Now they have come into this new land and fight on strange territory against those who are familiar with it. They face worse than they can imagine—but if that truth is told them they will not believe it."

Fors made no comment and after a moment the Star Captain went on:

"Langdon was my good friend always, but there was a streak of rashness in him and he did not always see the road ahead with clear eyes—"

At this criticism of his father Fors stirred but he did not speak.

"You have already, youth that you are, broken the clan laws—going your own way in pride and stubbornness—"

"I ask for nothing of the Eyrie's giving!"

"That is as it may be. I have twice heard your tale— you have a liking for this Arskane, I think. And you have eyes and a talent for getting under the skin of a man. This Marphy is one whom we might well remember. But Cantrul is a fighting man and of a different breed. Give him something to fight and he may be more open to other thoughts when the victory lies behind him. Very well, it is up to us to give him something to fight—something other than this tribe!"

"What—?" Fors brought only the one word out of his vast amazement.

"Beast Things. A well-baited trail could lead them north to the Plains camp."

Fors began to guess what was coming. He swallowed, his mouth and throat suddenly dry. To be bait for the Beast Things, to run north a pace or two before the most hideous death he knew—

"Such a task could be only ours alone—"

"You mean—not tell Lanard?"

"It would be best not. The plan would have no merit in their eyes now. You—you are an outlaw—a stranger who might well have little stomach for a fight not his. If you were to desert this camp, run away—"

Fors' nails bit into the palms of his balled fists. To appear a skin-saving coward in Arskane's eyes—just because Jarl had dreamed up so wild a plan— And yet part of him acknowledged the point of the Star Captain's reasoning.

"If the Plainsmen and this tribe fight—then it may well follow that the Beast Things shall finish off both of them."

"You do not have to point it out to me as one and one are two," Fors spat out.

Somewhere a childish voice was humming. And the brother of that child had brought him whole out of the valley of the lizards.

"When do I march?" he asked the Star Captain, hating him and every word he himself spoke.

16

※ **The Hunted and the Hunters**

AGAIN FORS WAS GRATEFUL FOR the mutation which had given him the keenness of his night sight. For almost an hour he had been wriggling down an ancient roadside ditch as a hanger-on of the small party of dark-skinned warriors whom Arskane now led. The broken surface of the nearby road was steel bright in the beams of the full moon, but he was sure that only he could see clearly what passed in the shadows beyond.

He was glad for the weight of bow and quiver across his shoulders—although the bow was the short, double-stringed weapon of the southerners and not the long one he was accustomed to. However, one sword was much like another and the new one at his belt already fitted his hand as if it had been forged to rest therein.

If it had not been for Jarl's plan he could have been really happy in that hour. To follow Arskane as one of his own tribe—to be accepted without question by those around him— But he was now pledged to put an end to that by his own actions—as soon as the time was right. Jarl was scouting to the west, the same compulsion driving him. They might be able to rendezvous after their break away from the tribe or they might never see each other again. Fors sent a silent call to Lura. If they did strike out into the wilderness tonight he would have to depend upon her wits and instinct—even more than upon his own.

The old road curved around the base of a rise. Fors stopped—had he really seen a flicker of movement in a bush halfway up that hill? His hand fell on the ankle of the man before him and he pressed hard, knowing that that signal would be as swiftly passed down the line.

That flash of cream white, that must be Lura crossing the road and heading up. But what he had caught only the faintest glimpse of had been far above that. Lura should rout it out—

There was a sudden scurry on the slope and Fors saw the outline of a crouching body. The sharp line of the thing's shoulders was only too familiar.

"Beast Thing!"

Lura's scream tore through the air drowning out the warning he shouted. The bushes threshed wildly at her attack. But she had had her instructions, not to kill now—only to harry and drive. The black thing snapped up out of hiding, arms flailing as the men around Fors went to their knees, arrows ready on strings. A cloud of feathered shafts flew. Most, Fors guessed, had fallen woefully short. Shooting up slope was always a tricky business.

The Beast Thing scuttled away over the crown of the hill at a desperate speed. And it was gone before other arrows could follow the first volley. Arskane edged along the line of disappointed archers to join Fors.

"Was that a scout?" he asked.

"Could be. They have always hunted in packs before. If it was a scout, it will now report."

Arskane chewed the tip of his thumb thoughtfully. Fors knew the worries which plagued him now. Ambush—that was the worst fear. They knew so little of the tactics of

he Beast Things—but lying in wait in the dark seemed to
fit the nature of the foul creatures best. In the ruined cit-
es they had always fought from cover when they could.

In the end Arskane did as Fors thought he would, gave
he signal to push on until they reached the boundaries of
their beat, one of the hills where the beacon had been
heaped some days before. So they crawled on, Lura
flanking the line of march. And they reached the beacon
hill without interference. Once there, Arskane formally
relieved the guard on duty.

The hour was close to dawn. A thin gray light gave ordinary trees and bushes a queer new life as if they were
now cut off from the real world by some flimsy barrier.
The beacon keepers had torn out or hacked away most of
the brush and saplings, so that the crown of the hill was
bare and one could see for a good range on all sides.

Fors located the camp by the river first and then set
about noting other landmarks which might help him keep
the proper course if he decided to make the break north
soon. The men whom they had relieved were marching in
fairly good order down the hill, ready to drop into the
protection of the road ditch, when the last one in that line
threw up his arms with a startled jerk and fell without a
sound. The man nearest him spun around just in time to
see him fall and started back to his aid, only to choke and
go to his knees tearing at the dart quivering in his own
throat.

They broke and ran back. But before they could reach
the miserable shelter afforded by the beacon, two more
died, Beast Thing steel in their contorted bodies. Only
one lived to break through to the men above.

And they, arrows ready, stood cursing, unable to shoot
at a foe which would not show itself.

Lura bounded out of cover below. She crowded up to
Fors, her blue eyes wide. Once getting his attention her
head swung meaningly from side to side. So, they were
surrounded! Maybe it was already too late to play the

game Jarl had set him. But even as that hope leaped he knew that he would have no escape—that this was jus the right sort of background for his break through—tha this would truly bring the Beast Things out on any trail he laid for them. He must openly desert Arskane—perhaps even to the southerner's death!

"We are surrounded." Tonelessly he passed on Lura': report.

Arskane nodded. "That I thought when she came to us. Well, now we may be forced to the waiting game." He turned to the men around him. "Down on your bellies. Crawl to the brush. We are clear targets to them now."

But before those orders were out of his mouth, the man beside him gave a gasping cry and held out his arm, a dart embedded in its flesh. As one man they moved into what cover they could find, Arskane pulling the wounded tribesman with him. But the cover of the beacon was a sorry shield.

The worst was not being able to sight the enemy. If they had been able to fight back it would not have been such a strain on the nerves. Picked and seasoned warriors knew better than to waste arrows on empty tree glades where nothing moved. It would be a battle in which patience would mean the most.

Fors sent Lura on another scouting trip. He must learn if there was any gap in the line the Beast Things held. If there was he should cross, break out to start north. If he won through they would probably wait to see if he headed for the river camp before they followed. So he must give the impression from the first that he was confused—then the sport of driving him might draw a portion of them after him.

During the morning there were two more casualties. Arskane, on making the rounds from one hidden man to another, found one dead with a dart pinning him down, and another with a torn leg, bandaging his own wound. When he came back to Fors he was very sober.

"At noon the camp will send us relief. If we light the beacon in warning they will prepare to move camp and that may lead them straight into an ambush. But Karson thinks he remembers something of the old smoke talk and he has volunteered to try it. Only those who signal will be exposed to fire." The southerner scowled at the silent woods. "We are but five now and two of those wounded. If we die and the tribe is saved—what does it matter?"

Fors fought his impulse to volunteer. He was sensitive to the slight hesitation with which Arskane regarded him when he did not answer. Then the southerner turned and crawled to the center of the beacon. Fors stirred. He might have gone after his companion had he not caught sight of something else which brought him into a crouch, tense and ready. Lura's head showed for the slightest instant below. She had found the gap he had sent her to search for. Now he, too, began to work his way around the hill to a point just above that section.

His dash would lead him across an open space and he must not be brought down. If he could time it right his move might draw fire which would otherwise be concentrated on the men at the beacon. He licked dry lips. Bow and quiver must be left behind, leaving him only sword and hunting knife.

Yes, he had not been mistaken. Lura's brown ears showed again in outline against a moss-grown rock. She was waiting for him. He gathered his feet under him, and, as an arrow from a bow, he dashed out of cover and zigzagged down the slope. There was a single shout of surprise from behind and then he was into the woods, Lura with him.

Now he was absorbed in the task at hand. He burst through a screen of small trees, making only the most elementary effort to hide his trail. Lura's warning that they were now followed set his heart to pounding. Now—now it was just his own two feet, his hunting lore, and his sense of direction against all the cunning of the enemy.

He must be a tempting morsel always just about to fall into the pursuers' hands, and yet he must keep from capture and lead the run into Plains territory so that Cantrul might be provoked into action. As Jarl had outlined it the plan was as simple as it was deadly—but was it going to work?

There were short periods during the rest of the day when he could snatch some rest, always after Lura assured him that something still ran the trail behind. Once he dared verify that for himself, having climbed a cliff after crossing a stream. He lingered in a shallow crevice at the top long enough to see three gray shapes come out of the woods a half mile back, the first on all fours sniffing the ground as it came.

Three—out of how many? But the beacon must have warned the camp. He must think of nothing else now but his own task. If ever his eyes and ears served him well they must do better than that now. As a fugitive gaining his second wind perhaps he would dare display a little more cunning. The Beast Things might accept the idea that sheer panic had brought him away from the beacon, but that would not prevent a greater show of caution now. He tried several of the simpler trail-hiding tricks and waited for Lura's verdict. It was favorable, the chase was still on.

Some hours before evening he struck west, trying to intercept a line which must run to the beaver lake and so to Cantrul's camp—unless the fire had driven the Plainsmen from that base. He ate as he went, berries and handfuls of ripe grain pulled from the ragged self-sown patches in the old fields. There were hard, half-ripe peaches in an old orchard he pounded through and he had enough to keep him going when washed down with water from brook and spring.

The night was the worst. He had to lay up for rest, swinging into the branches of a tree, close enough to an outcrop of rock to be able to leap away if the need came.

Lura catnapped on that rock, her brown and cream melting into the weathered stone. He dozed and woke, to stretch cramped muscles and doze again. Before morning he moved twice, putting a mile between each resting place and choosing each for the ability to make a quick retreat.

When the gray of dawn caught him again he was lying flat on a bluff overhanging a stream he was sure was the outlet of the beaver lake. Pieces of charred wood caught among the boulders below proved that. The size of the stream had dwindled, perhaps the beavers had started repairs in the broken dam. Fors lay there, every aching joint, every exhausted muscle protesting the move he was willing his body into making. It was as if he had been running for days—since they had left the ruined city they had been on the move with little or no rest. And none to look for in the immediate future either—

Luckily he was facing downstream, with his eyes on the moving surface, for now he saw what might have been the strangest sight to ever appear on that forgotten shore. An animal was swimming up river, nosing along the bank in a peculiar fashion, almost as if it were intelligently questing. When it reached the spot between two stones where Fors had knelt to drink before he climbed, it scrambled out of the water and sat up on its haunches, its forepaws held close to its lighter underbelly, its head high with sniffing nose testing the flowing air currents.

It was a rat—one of the huge, gray-coated ones of the old breed with which man has fought eternal warfare since the first days of time. A rat— Fors remembered back to the sunny morning in the ruins of the old city shops when just such a beast had sat to watch him without alarm. The rats flourished in the cities—everyone knew that. But for the most part men did not see them— even there. Their ways were underground, in the noisome burrows they had hollowed and claimed from cellar to cellar, through the old sewers and waterways.

The rat shook itself. Then the growing light brought a

flash from its throat as it raised higher its head. A metal collar—surely that was a metal collar. But a collar on a rat—why—who—

Who lived in the cities? Who might tame and use rats? He knew the answer to that. But why? The rat alone was not a formidable fighter—not an ally as good as Lura—they were only to be feared in hordes. Hordes—!

The rat jumped to the top of a boulder and began to lick itself dry, as if it had successfully completed a set task and could now take time for its own concerns. Fors had not been mistaken by some trick of the light—as the beast's head twisted and turned the collar was easy to see. It was made of flat links and seemed flexible.

Suddenly the creature stopped its toilet and crouched very still, its beady eyes aimed downstream. Fors could not move. He had to see what was going to happen. And the same idea flashed to his mind from Lura who was flattened out against the rock some feet away, her lips frozen in a snarl.

They heard the splashing first, a sound too regular to be natural. If he were wise he would leave now, but he could not.

An ungainly figure came skittering through the shallows around the waterworn rocks. Its shape was queer but Fors peered until he made out that the hunched back of the creature was in reality a basket cage. At its coming the collared rat showed its teeth wickedly but it did not attempt to escape.

The Beast Thing came on, leisurely reached out a long arm and picked up the rat by its collar while it snapped its teeth and clawed wildly. With the ease of long practice the rat master threw his captive through a trap door into the cage and snapped it shut again. From the wild chattering which ensued Fors deduced that more than one rat rode therein. But Lura was gliding away from her vantage point and he knew that she was right. It was time for them to go.

But as he fled he continued to wonder. Why the rats? Unless the Beast Things had rested and sent the rats to trail him during the night. If that was true his taking to the trees must have baffled them for a good while. Or did rats climb? He wished that he knew more about their habits. And why had none of the Star Men discovered during their brushes with the Beast Things this use of rats? Was it new—another manifestation of the urge which was bringing the sub-human forces out of their century old burrows to challenge the descendants of the Old Ones?

All the old tales about the Beast Things went through his head as he mechanically set a trail which would delay but not altogether throw off the pursuers. They were supposed to be the offspring of city dwellers caught in the full strength of the radiation waves, children so much mutant in form and mind that they were no longer human at all. That was one explanation.

But there was another story about them too. And that was that the Beast Things were the descendants of companies of the invading enemy, parties of soldiers both male and female who had been landed to occupy the country and then been forgotten when their own nation had disappeared under retaliatory atom bombing. Soldiers, bewildered and totally lost when no orders came, who clung stubbornly to the positions they had been sent to occupy—remaining there in spite of the radiation. Whichever theory was the true one, the Beast Things, though they aroused revulsion and instinctive hatred among the humans, were also victims of the Old Ones' tragic mistake, as shattered in their lives as the cities had been.

Fors jogged into the first section of the fire-swept land. Ahead lay a black and desolate waste. And there was little or no cover left. He would have to dare discovery from the rat-carrying Beast Thing and take to the riverside again.

The smell of burnt stuff was thick in the air, the stench making him cough as much as the powdery ashes which drifted up between his feet. Perhaps it was best to take to water. Here and there a fallen tree still showed a heart of glowing coals.

Coughing, rubbing his eyes to clear them, Fors scrambled over rocks and once even swam to breast the current. Here water marks were high above the present level of the stream. It was evident that the dam must have been at least partly repaired.

Then he clambered up over that structure itself. Before him lay the lake, ringed completely around with the black scar of fire. The beavers faced a famine season unless they moved. It would be a full year before the saplings would begin to sprout again and not for several generations would trees stand tall there once more.

Fors dove into the water. Even here the smell of smoke and the tang of burning clung. There were bodies floating too, a deer, a wild cow, and close to the far shore, a horse bearing on its puffed flank the painted sign of the Plains camp. He swam by it and headed up the feeder stream down which he and Arskane had won to freedom. But before he left the lake he glanced back.

And over the beaver dam was clambering the hunch-backed figure of the rat carrier. Behind it three others came up. As they hesitated on the dam, teetering as if they feared either the water or the still smoldering footing offered ashore, five more of their kind appeared.

Fors drew back into a half circle of rocks. Jarl's plan had succeeded. He had no way of guessing how many of the Beast Things had ambushed the party at the beacon hill, but the pack now running at his heels had numbers enough to interest Cantrul. The Beast Things were dour and terrible fighters, and they were fighters who never wanted to head an open attack. Their present openness showed how much they held him in contempt. Fors watched, to see the rat cage unstrapped while its bearer went over into the lake.

A comrade tore away part of the dam's substance to make a raft to carry the cage. Then they were all swimming, clumsily but surely, taking turns pushing the cage before them.

Fors took to his heels, skidding over slime-coated stones, the stream rising from thigh to waist as he panted through it and tried to dodge the smoking timber which had fallen across the banks here and there.

The patch of green grass he sighted where he had come to expect only the black of the burning was almost a shock. But there were reeds standing tall and unscorched in a thick mass. He plunged through them to shore. The mud bank beyond was thickly scored with hoofprints, some still fresh, good evidence that the Plainsmen were still there. Lura's tracks overlay the others and the marks of her claws on the clay overhang were deep. Fors grabbed for the tough roots of the bush and pulled himself up.

He pulled himself up and took two steps. Then he tripped and rolled, his feet jerked out from under him. And as he went down he heard the shrilling of a vicious laughter. His hand was tight on his sword hilt and he had the blade out almost before he had again sucked the air into his lungs. He came up, the bare blade in swing, ready and waiting.

17

※   **The Last War**

FORS SAW WHAT HE KNEW would be there—a ring of wiry
gray bodies around him. The Beast Things must have
been concealed in the grass. A little beyond him, Lura—
also a captive—threshed, the noose tight about her neck
as she clawed up great patches of turf in her struggle for
freedom.

Another jerk on the trapping cord brought him
sprawling forward to the accompaniment of inhuman
laughter. There was only one thing he could do now.
Without trying to regain his feet or even to get to his
knees, Fors struggled across the ground on his belly to
Lura, a move which seemed to take his captors entirely
by surprise. None of them could prevent his sword biting
through the cord which strangled her. And his order had
flashed from mind to mind in that same instant.

"Find Nag—and he who hunts with Nag—find!"

She would be more likely to join the other cat than go
directly to Jarl. But where the black cat ran the Star Captain would not be far away.

Lura's powerful legs gathered under her. Then she

sprang in a great arching leap, passing over the head of one of the Beast Things. Free of their circle she went as a streak of light fur into the grass and was lost. Fors took advantage of the excitement to slash at the tangle of cord about his ankles and he had one foot free before the rage of the Beast Things flamed and they concentrated again on the remaining captive.

There was no hope now. He wondered how many seconds of life he had before he would go down for the last time, pin-cushioned by the darts they all held. But—when in doubt—attack! The advice Langdon had once given him stiffened his sword arm now. Speed— Do as much harm as he could. There was no chance of keeping alive until Lura found Jarl but he could take some of these beasts with him.

With the same lithe speed Lura had displayed he sprang at one of the circle, blade up and ready to twist in the vicious thrust which was the most dangerous he knew. And almost he made it, had his one foot not remained in bond. As it was he laid open gray hide, not in the deep death-dealing gash he had planned, but in a shallow cut which ran red half across the thing's bulbous paunch.

He ducked the blow aimed at his head, ducked and struck up again. Then his sword arm went limp, the blade falling out of his numbed fingers as a dart went home. A cuff delivered across the side of his face before he could raise his left hand sent him sailing back surrounded by a burst of red which turned into black nothingness.

Pain dragged him back, a red agony of pain which ran through his veins like fire, a fire which ran from his torn arm. He tried to move feebly and found that his ankles and wrists were fast—he had been tied down, spread-eagled to stakes in the ground.

It was hard to get his eyes open, the left eyelid was glued to his cheek. But now he was looking up into the sky. So he was not dead yet, he thought dully. And since the tree he could see was green he must still be close to the point where he had been captured. He tried to raise his head, had one moment of blurred sight, and then was so sick that he dropped it flat again and shut his eyes to hide reeling sky and heaving ground.

Later there was noise—much of it which rang in his head until he forced his eyes open again. Beast Things were driving up another prisoner. By his hair dress he was a Plainsman. And he was sent flat with a blow and pegged out beside Fors. The Beast Things favored him with a couple of rib-cracking kicks before they left, making suggestions in gestures—suggestions which did not promise well for the future.

Fors' head felt thick and tight, he could not force his thoughts together in the fog which seemed to gather in his brain. It was better just to lie still and endure the pain in his arm as best he could.

A shrill squeaking pulled him out of the fog of pain and sickness. He turned his head to see the wicker baskets of rats a few feet away. The Beast Thing who had worn it on its back gave a sigh of relief as it dropped its burden and joined the three or four of its fellows who were lounging under a nearby tree. Their guttural greeting meant nothing to Fors.

But through the open slits of the basket cage he fancied he could see sparks of reddish light—small wicked eyes watching him with a horrid kind of intelligence. All at once the rats were quiet, save when at intervals one or another squeaked briefly as if making some comment to its companions.

How long did they watch each other? Time in true measure no longer existed for Fors. After a space the Beast Things made a fire and broiled ragged pieces of meat, some still backed with horsehide. When the scent of that reached the rats they went wild, running about their cage until it rocked, squeaking at the tops of their thin voices. But none of their masters made any move to share the feast with them.

When one was done it came over to the cage and shook it, yelling. The rats were quiet, again their eyes showed at the open spaces, looking now only at the prisoners—red eyes, angry, hungry eyes.

Fors tried to tell himself that what he suspicioned was not true, that in his torment he had no control over imagination. Surely that Beast Thing had not made a promise then—a promise which Fors dared not believe lest he lose all control over wits and will.

But those red rat eyes watched and watched. He could see the sharp claws pointing between the wicker ribs, and the gleam of teeth— And always the watching eyes—

By the lengthening shadow he guessed that it was far along in the afternoon when the third and last party of Beast Things came into camp. And with them was the leader.

He was no taller than other members of his tribe, but a certain arrogant confidence in his bearing and stride made him seem to overtop the others. His hairless head was narrow with the same slit nose and protruding fanged jaws, but the brain case was domed, larger by half again over any of the rest. His eyes held a cunning intelligence and there was a subtle difference in the way he looked over his world—a difference which Fors did not miss. This Beast Thing was no true man—no, but neither was he as brutish as the pack he led. One could almost believe that here lay the power which had brought the foul band out to range the open lands.

Now he came to stand between the two captives. Fors turned away from the rat cages to meet those queer eyes firmly.

But the mountaineer could read nothing understandable in their depths and the protruding jaws expressed no emotion which might be deduced by a human. The leader of the Beast Things might have been wildly elated, annoyed, or merely curious, as he stared at first one and then the other of the staked-out prisoners. But curiosity must have directed his next move for he dropped down crosslegged between them and mouthed the first real words Fors had ever heard issue from one of the city-bred monsters.

"You—where?" He demanded that of the Plainsman who could not or would not answer.

When he did not reply the Beast Leader leaned over and, with a deliberation which was as cruel as the blow, slapped the captive with lip-bursting force across the mouth. It then swung to Fors and repeated his question.

"From the south—" Fors croaked.

"South," the leader repeated, distorting the word oddly. "What in south?"

"Men—many, many men. Ten tens of tens—"

But that sum was either beyond the calculations of the creature beside him, or the Beast Thing did not believe in its truth, for it cackled with a ghastly travesty of laughter and, reaching out, brought a fist down across his wounded arm. Fors fainted, dropping into blackness with a sick swoop.

A scream brought him back to consciousness. He had the echoes of that cry still ringing through his head when he forced open his eyes and tried to stabilize crazily flowing blocks of light and shade. A second cry of pain and horror settled the world into place.

The leader of the Beast Things still squatted between the captives and in outstretched hand it held the struggling body of one of the hungry rats. There was red on the vermin's fangs and more scarlet drops spattered its breast and forepaws as it fought like a mad thing against the hold which kept it from its prey.

Down the arm and side of the Plainsman a line of dripping gashes told the story. His distorted face was a mask of tortured despair as he cursed, his words a frenzied mumble which soared into a scream every time the Beast Leader held the rat closer.

But a cry of pure rage cut through the captive's breathless sobbing, a cry uttered by the leader. The rat had turned to slash one of the fingers which held it. With a snarl the Beast Leader twisted the writhing body. There was a cracking and the thing he threw from him was limp and broken. He got to his feet, the torn finger at his mouth.

A respite—for how long? The Beast Things seemed to feel themselves safe in this camping site they had chosen. They were not moving on for the night—but just as Fors decided that, the picture changed suddenly. Two more of the enemy came out of the bush and between them they pulled along a mangled, trodden body—the body of one of their own kind. Over this there was a hasty consultation and then the leader barked an order. The bearer of the rat cage took up its burden and four of the largest of its fellows came over to the captives.

Knives slashed free their bonds and they were pulled and slapped to their feet. When it was apparent that neither could walk, there was a second conference. From gestures Fors gathered that one party was in favor of killing them at once, but that the leader opposed this. And in the end the leader carried the debate. Two of the clan trotted off and returned shortly with stout saplings which were trimmed of branches. And in a moment or two Fors found himself lashed to one of these, dangling face to the ground, carried between two of the Beasts who moved on with their deceptively easy pace.

He never remembered much of that night. The bearers of his pole changed from time to time, but he swung in a daze, rousing only when he was dropped painfully to the ground during these operations. And they must have been halted for some time when he became aware of the sound.

He was on the ground, his ear tight to the earth. And at first he thought that the pounding beat he heard must be the heated blood running in his own feverish body—or else that it was but another shadowy bit of a delirious nightmare. But it continued—steadily—alive—alive, and somehow reassuring. Once, long before, he had heard a sound like that—it had had a meaning. But the meaning was lost. Now he was only aware of his body, the mass of pain which had become a thing apart from Fors. Fors was gone away—far away from that pain—what remained could not think—could only feel and endure.

Why, now the distant throbbing was broken by another, a deeper, heavier beat—two sounds. And he had once known them both. But neither mattered now. He must watch red eyes which stared at him from spaces in wickerwork, red, hungry eyes which watched and waited, growing still more starved and demanding. And in the end those eyes would come closer and closer and teeth would be with them. But that did not matter very much either.

Somewhere there was shouting, it tore a hole through his head, made his ears ring. But it did not frighten the eyes, they still watched and waited.

The throbbing, now it filled the air, beating into him. Why, he was up now, being held on his feet by rough hands. He was being tied fast again—or so he thought, he was too numb to feel bonds. But he was standing right enough, looking down from the crest of a hill.

And he watched the dream roll on—the dream which had nothing to do with him. There were horsemen down there, riding in a charging wave. Around and around they were circling. He closed his eyes to the glare of light. Around and around—almost they were passing in answer to the beat—almost but not quite. The beat was not coming from the horsemen—it had another source.

Fors hung unresisting. But a tiny spark of the real Fors was moving in the broken, hurting body. Now he forced open his eyes and there was intelligence and purpose looking out of them.

The horsemen were keeping in their moving circle and as they rode they hurled spears up the grade. But among the horsemen others tramped now, men who ran lightly with ready bows. And the arrows made a cloud against the sun. The noose of men and horses drew smaller and tighter about the hill.

Then Fors realized suddenly that his body was part of the defense wall of those besieged here, that he had been fastened up for a screen behind which the dart throwers could crouch in safety. And those darts, expertly aimed, were taking toll below. Man and horse went down to cry and kick or lie still. But that did not halt the circle, nor deaden the flying arrows.

Once there was a loud screech of anguish and a body fell out from behind the barrier of which he was a part. On hands and knees it blundered downhill, heading for one of the nimble archers. They met in a headlong crash of fighting rage. Then a horseman swung low from the saddle and used his lance expertly. Both bodies lay still as he rode on.

A heavy blow landed on Fors' side. He forgot about the fighting as he looked down. His own arm hung there, free, a dead weight with the cut thong still ringing the purple swollen wrist. Arrow or spear had cut that tie. He ceased to have any interest in the battle—his world narrowed in that instant to the one free hand. In the puffed flesh there was no feeling, he could not even move it yet. So he concentrated on the fingers, he must move his thumb, his forefinger—even a fraction of an inch—he must!

There! He could have shouted at his success. The arm still was limp and heavy against his side but he had clawed the fingers against his thigh. One hand and arm free—and it was his right—the unhurt one! He turned his head. His other wrist was fast to another sapling post driven into the ground. But the very way the Beast Things were using him, as part of their defense works, was now in his favor. The left arm was not stretched full length from his shoulder. If he could bring the right fingers up, bring them up and make them work, he was sure he could unfasten that one too.

The barrier of which he was now a part must have screened his actions from his captors—or else they were too occupied to take any interest in him. He was able to bring the hand across, bring it across and force the fingers to the bonds on his left wrist. But it was another thing to untie the cords there. His numb fingers could not even feel and they kept slipping off.

He fought against his own stubborn and mistreated flesh, fought a battle as hard as the one raging about him. Arrows thudded home inches away, one of the spears brought a gasp of pain from him as the shaft struck full across his skin, but he willed his hand to the work. The torture of returning circulation hit full, but he made himself think only of those painful fingers and what he must have the courage and patience to make them do.

Then, all at once, something gave. He held an end of loose hide and his left arm fell inert as he gritted his teeth against the pain brought by that sudden release. But there was no time to nurse it now, he went down to the ground. In their haste the Beast Things had set but one loop of the hide around his ankles. He sawed at it with the edge of an arrowhead until it parted.

It would be safer to stay where he was for the moment. The Beast Things could not get at him without climbing the barrier and thus exposing themselves. And, flat to the ground as he was, he might escape the worst of the hail from below. So, too shaky to move or even to think clearly, he continued to cower where he had fallen.

After a space of time Fors was aware of another sound, coming through the din. He turned his head a fraction of an inch and was face to face with the rat cage. It, too, had been added to the breastworks. And the prisoners within it were racing about, their frenzied squeaking born of fear and hate loud enough to reach his ears. The sight of those obscene, too plump bodies aroused him as nothing else could have done and he hitched away from the swaying cage.

Where was the other prisoner—the Plainsman? Fors levered up cautiously on his elbows to see some distance away a fallen head and limp body. He allowed his head to sink back on his arms. He could move now—after a fashion—both legs and one arm would obey him. He could roll down the hill—

But that Plainsman—still exposed to certain death—

Fors began to creep, past the cage of rats, past a bundle of brush, a lopsided, hastily planted stockade of saplings, past the stuff the Beast Things had grabbed up and thrown together in an attempt to keep out arrows and spears. He traveled only a few inches at a time and there were long pauses between those inches. But he gained ground.

A dart struck the earth just beyond his straining hand. The Beast Things were aware of him at last and were trying to bring him down. But the one who exposed itself in such a try fell back choking, an arrow through its throat. It was not wise to give the archers below even a partial target. Fors crawled on.

He was confident now that he could reach the Plainsman. And he paid no attention to what chanced below or inside the stockade. He must save all strength and will for his journey.

Then he was squatting at a pair of bound ankles—reaching up for knots which held torn wrists. But his hands fell back. Two arrows held the captive pinned more securely than any hide rope. The Plainsman would never need help now.

Fors sank onto the rough trampled soil. The will and purpose which had driven him went out as strength of body flows out of an open wound. He could feel them ebbing and he did not care.

Mountain rocks rose up about him and across crags the gray flags of a storm flew their tatters. He could hear the howl of wind down one of the narrow valleys, see the gathering of the black clouds. It must be winter for those were snow clouds. It would be well to head back to the protection of the Eyrie—back to the fires and stout stone walls—before those winds bit and the snow fell.

Back to the Eyrie. He did not know that he was on his feet now—no more than he knew that behind him there came cries of consternation and red rage as the Beast Thing leader went down to death under a chance arrow. Fors did not know that he was tottering down the slope, his empty hands out, while over the barrier behind him boiled a rabble of maddened, long-armed things intent on taking vengeance with fangs and claws, blind now to the precaution which had kept them safe.

Fors was walking a mountain trail and Lura was behind him. She had caught his hand in her mouth to lead him—which was right for the snow or the wind was blinding him and it was hard to keep on the trail. But the Eyrie lay just ahead and Langdon was waiting for him. Tonight they would study together that tiny scrap of map—a map of a city which lay on the shores of a lake. Langdon was going to put that map to the test soon. And after he, Fors, had been accepted by the Star Men he would also follow old maps—follow and find—

His hand went uncertainly to his head. Lura was hurrying him so. She wanted the fire and the meat. It was not right to keep Langdon waiting. Because somewhere there was a city waiting, too, a city of tall towers and filled storehouses, cracked roads and forgotten wonders. He must tell Langdon all about it. But that was not right— the city belonged to Langdon—not to him. He had never seen a ruined city. The storm must be making him lightheaded.

He staggered, one of the Beast Things aimed a blow at him as it passed to join the fighting mob below.

So many rocks—he had trouble keeping to his feet among these rocks. He'd best be careful. But he was going home. There were the fires—showing brightly through

he dark. And Lura still held his hand. If the wind would
only die down a little—the sound of it was wild and
strange—almost like the battle cries of an army. But there
tood the Eyrie—right there—

18

A New Star Shines

IT WAS LATE AFTERNOON. Smoke curled up from a ceremonial fire. Fors looked downslope to where green grass had been ground into a pulp by the pressure of many feet. And that pulp was stained with stale splotches of red. But the men below were squatting unconcernedly on it—their eyes only for each other. Two lines—facing across the fire warily—weapons unsheathed and to hand. Between those lines were the chieftains of the tribes. But both sides bore the scars of a hard fight and there were holes in the ranks which would never be filled again.

Fors forgot his own bruises as he watched Arskane step into place at the right of his father. The woman chief who had given the mountaineer the rights of the tribe was there, too, her robe a spark of bright color among the drabness of the hide jerkins and the tanned skins of the men.

And opposed was Marphy and his fellow long robe. Only Cantrul was missing. The heads of family clans had usurped the place the High Chief should have held.

"Cantrul—?"

From beside Fors, Jarl made answer to that half question.

"Cantrul was a warrior—and as a warrior he entered on the long trail in a fitting fashion—taking a goodly number of the enemy with him. They have not yet raised up a new High Chief in his place."

What else the Star Captain might have added was blotted out in a roll from the talking drums, a roll which wrung harsh echoes from the surrounding hills. And when those faded, Lanard edged forward, though he needs must lean upon the arm of his son to spare weight from a leg which was bandaged from knee to ankle.

"Ho—warriors!" His voice followed the drums' beat in its force. "Here have we carried spears to a great killing and given the death birds a feast beyond the memory of our fathers' fathers! From the south have we marched to this war and victory is ours. Our arrows have struck full upon their marks and our swords have been blooded to their hilts. Is this not so, my brothers?"

And out from the ranks of his tribe behind him came a low growl of agreement. Here and there some of the younger men cried the shrill war slogan of a family clan.

But from the ranks of the under chieftains in the mass of the Plainspeople arose another man and he answered with prideful words of his own:

"Lances bite as deep as swords, and the Plainsmen have never known fear of a fight. Death birds eat today from our providing also. We stand shame-filled in the sight of no man!"

Someone began the war song Fors had heard on his night of captivity among the tents. Hands were reaching for bows and lances. Fors got to his feet, forcing his body to obey his will. He pushed aside the hand the Star Captain put out to stay him.

"There is a fire breaking out here," he said slowly. "If it comes to full flame it may eat us all up. Let me go—!"

But as he half staggered down the slope to the council fire, he sensed that the Star Captain was still at his back.

"You have fought!"

From somewhere within him that clear cold voice had come at his willing— It was a chill wind to cut through the evil vapors of a swampland. In his head the thoughts Arskane had planted long ago were coming to life so clearly that he was confident at last of their truth and rightness.

"You have fought!"

"Ahhh—" That answering sound was close to the purr which Lura might voice when remembering her hunt.

"You have fought," he repeated for the third time and knew that he had them now. "The Beast Things are dead. *These* Beast Things—"

That accented word had riveted their full attention.

"You have looked upon the enemy slain—is that not so? Well, I have lain in their hands—and the horror that you know is tenfold in my memory. But I say that you might also look in fear as well as in pride of your victory, for there lies among them a dire promise. My fathers' fathers fought with these creatures—when still they held to their home burrows. My father died under their claws and fangs. Long have we known them. But now there has been born amongst them something stronger—something which threatens us as the burrow creepers of old never did. Ask it of your wise men, warriors. Ask them what they found in the circle of the dead within that barrier up there—what may come again to plague us in future years. Tell these your people, oh, healer of bodies." He addressed himself to the Plains white robe. "And you, oh, Lady." He spoke to the woman chief. "What have you seen?"

It was the woman who replied first.

"I saw and heard many things. In the seeing there was nothing to doubt. I hope with all my heart that your conjectures are mistaken. There lay among the Beast dead ne who was different. And if the fates are against us, hen this one will be born again among them—again and again. And, its knowledge being greater, so will it prove a worse menace to us and all human beings. Thus, because his may be true, I say that those who are humankind must stand together and put a united sword wall against hese things bred out of the ancient evil of the cities which was sown by the Old Ones—"

"It is true that mutants may come of mutant stock." The white robe spoke after her almost against his will. "And these Beast Things were led and ordered as never has their race been before. When their strange chief fell they were broken, as if their knowledge was all blotted out in that single death. If they breed more such as he, then they shall prove a force we must reckon with. We know but little of these creatures and what their powers may be. How can we guess now what we shall be called to go up against a year, ten years, a generation from now? This land is wide and there may be much hiding within its vastness which is a menace to our breed—"

"The land is wide," Fors repeated. "What do you and your tribe seek for here, Lanard?"

"A homeland. We search out a place to build our houses and sow our fields anew, to pasture our sheep and dwell in peace. After the burning mountains and quaking land drove us forth from the valley of our fathers—the sacred place where their machines landed from the sky at the end of the Old Ones' war—we have wandered many circles of the seasons. Now in these wide fields, along the river, we have found what we have sought for so long. And no man or beast shall drive us from it!" As he ended, his hand was on his sword hilt and he stared straight along the ranks of the Plainsmen.

Fors turned now to Marphy: "And what do your people seek, Marphy of the plains?"

The Recorder raised his eyes from the ground where a

pattern of crushed grass blades had apparently held his attention.

"Since the days of the Old Ones we of the Plains have been a roving people. First we were so because of the evil death which abode in the air of many quarters of the land, so that a man must be on the move to shun those places where plagues and the blue fires waited to slay him. We are now hunters and rovers and herdsmen, warriors who care not to be tied to any camp. It is in us to travel far, to seek new places and new hills standing high against the sky—"

"So." Fors let that one word fall into the silence of those war-torn ranks.

It was a long minute before he spoke again. "You," he pointed to Lanard, "wish to settle and build. That is your nature and way of life. You" —it was Marphy he turned to now— "would move, grazing your herds and hunting. These," he bent a stiff arm painfully to gesture up the hill to that uneven pile of earth and stone under which lay the bodies of the Beast Things, "live to destroy both of you if they can. And the land is wide . . ."

Lanard cleared his throat—the sound was sharp and loud. "We would live in peace with all who raise not the sword against us. In peace there is trade, and in trade there is good for all. When the winter closes and the harvest has been poor, then may trade save the life of a tribe."

"You are warriors and men," the woman chief of the Dark People broke in, her head high, her eyes straight as she measured the line of strangers facing her. "War is meat and drink at the table of men—yes—but it was that which brought the Old Ones down! War again, men, and you will destroy us utterly and we shall be eaten up and forgotten so that it shall be as if man had never lived to walk these fields—leaving our world to the holding of those!" She pointed to the Beast Things' mound. "If now we draw sword against one another then in our folly we hall have chosen the evil part for the last time, and it is better that we die quickly and this earth be clean of us!"

The Plainspeople were quiet until along the ranks of the men a murmur arose and it spread to where their women were gathered. And the voices of the women grew louder and stronger. From their midst arose one who must have ruled a chieftain's tent since there was gold binding her hair:

"Let there be no war between us! Let there be no more wailing of the death song among our tents! Say it loudly, oh, my sisters!" And her appeal was taken up by all the women, to be echoed until it became a chant as stirring as the war song.

"No more war! No more war between us!"

So did the cup of blood and brotherhood pass from chief to chief on the field and the ranks of the Dark Ones and the Plainsmen were made one by the ritual so that never again might man of one raise lance against man of the other.

Fors sank down upon a flat-topped rock. The strength which had upheld him drained away. He was very tired and the excitement beyond no longer had anything to do with him. He had no eyes for the melting of the stiff tribal lines and the mingling of clan and people.

"This is but a beginning!" He identified the quick eager voice of Marphy and looked around slowly, almost sullenly.

The Plainsman was talking to Jarl, gesturing, his eyes bright. But the Star Captain was his usual calm contained self.

"A beginning, yes, Marphy. But we still have much to master. If I may see those northern records of yours. We of the Star House have not penetrated that far—"

"Of course. And—" Marphy seemed hesitant before he plunged into his counter request— "that cage of rats. I have had it brought into my tent. There are three still alive and from them we may learn—"

Fors shivered. *He* had no desire to see those captives.

"You claim them as your spoil of war?"

Marphy laughed. "That I shall do. And other spoil beside the vermin shall we ask for—a greater gift from you. This fellow rover of yours—"

He touched gentle fingers to Fors' stooped shoulder. It seemed to the mountaineer that Jarl displayed a flash of surprise.

"This one has the gift of tongues and the mind which sees. He shall be a guide for us." Marphy's words spilled out as if now that he had a kindred spirit in which to confide he could no longer bottle his thoughts. "And in return we shall show him strange lands and far places. For it is in him to be a rover—even as are we—"

Jarl's fingers plucked at his lower lip: "Yes, rover was he born, and in him flows Plains blood. If he—"

"You forget." Fors did not force a smile this time. "I am mutant."

Before either man could answer someone else came up—Arskane. His face still bore the marks of the fight and he favored his shoulder as he moved. But when he spoke it was with an assumption of authority which he plainly did not expect to have disregarded.

"We break camp to march— I have come for my brother!"

Marphy bristled. "He rides with us!"

Fors' laugh had no humor in it. "Since I cannot travel on my feet I shall be a drag in any company—"

"We shall rig a pony litter," was Arskane's quick reply.

"There are also horse litters," began Marphy jealously.

Jarl moved. "It seems that you now have a choice to make," he observed dispassionately to Fors. For a moment it seemed to the younger mountain man that only the two of them were there. And neither Arskane nor Marphy pressed his claim farther.

Fors held his free hand to his swimming head. He had Plains blood from his mother—that was true. And the wild free life of the roving horsemen appealed to him. If he went with Marphy no secrets of the ruined country would be hidden from him now—he could learn much. He could make such maps as even the Star Men had never dreamed of possessing, see forgotten cities and loot them for his pleasure, always going on to new country beyond.

If he took the hand Arskane had half offered in support a few minutes ago he would be accepting brotherhood and the close-knit ties of a family clan such as he had never had. He would know all warmth of affection, and go to build a town, maybe in time a city, which would mark the first step back along the road the sins of the Old Ones had lost for their sons. It would be a hard life but, in its way, a rewarding one, as adventurous—though he would never rove far—as Marphy's.

But—there was the third road. And it ran from a choice he knew only too well. When he thought he was dying—back there during the battle—his feet had taken it without his will. It led to the rare coldness of the mountain heights, into the austere chill of punishment and hurt and eternal discouragement.

So when he raised his hand he dared not look at Arskane or Marphy, but he found and held Jarl's uncompromising eyes as he asked:

"Is it true that I am outlawed?"

"You have been called three times at the council fire."

He recognized flat truth and accepted it. But he had another question:

"Since I was not there to answer in my own voice I have the right of repeal for the period of six moons?"

"You have."

Fors picked at the sling which bound his left arm across his chest. There was an even chance that it would heal straight and strong again. The healer had promised him that after probing the wound.

"I think then," he found that he had to stop and work out his words, to regain discipline over his voice, "I shall go and claim that right. Six moons are not yet gone—"

The Star Captain nodded. "If you can travel in three days' time you will make it."

"Fors!" At that protest from Arskane, the mountaineer winced. But when he turned his head his voice still held firm.

"It was you yourself, brother, who spoke of duty once—"

Arskane's hand dropped. "Remember—we be brothers, you and I. Where lies my hearth—there is your place waiting." He went and did not look back, he was swallowed up in the throng of his tribesmen.

Marphy came to life. He shrugged. Already he was intent on other plans, other enthusiasms. But he lingered long enough to say:

"From this hour on for you there runs a mount in my herd and the promise of meat, and shelter in my tent. Look for the Standard of the Red Fox when you have need of aid, my young friend." His hand sketched a half salute as he strode away.

Fors spoke to the Star Captain: "I shall go—"

"With me. I have also a report to make to the tribe— we journey together."

Was that news good or otherwise? Under other circumstances Fors could have longed for no greater pleasure than to travel in the company of the Star Captain. But now he went in a manner as Jarl's prisoner. He sat glumly looking over the battlefield—only a small scrimmage— one which the Old Ones, with their fleets in the air and their armed columns on land, would not even have mentioned. Yet here a full-sized war had been fought and out of it had come an idea—perhaps one which would prove the starting point for men. It would be a long weary trail

or them to travel—the road back to such a world as the
Old Ones had known. And maybe not even the sons'
sons' sons of those who had fought here would live to see
more than the glimmerings of its beginning growth. Or
maybe the world which would come would be a better
world.

The Plainsmen and the Dark Ones were still suspicious,
still wary of one another. Soon the tribes would separate
for a space. But, perhaps in six months' time, a party of
Plainsmen would venture again to the south, to visit the
bend in the river and see with wondering eyes the cabins
which stood there. And one rider would trade a well-
tanned hide for a clay dish or a string of colored beads to
take home to astonish his women. Afterward would come
others, many others, and there would in time be marriages
between tent and cabin. And in fifty years—one nation.

"There will be one nation." Fors hunched on the riding
pad of the steady old horse Marphy had forced upon him.
Two days had sped but the tramped earth would show
scars for a long time.

Jarl shot a measuring glance over the field they
crossed.

"And how many years pass before such a miracle?" he
inquired with his old irony.

"Fifty—fifty years—perhaps—"

"If nothing intervenes to stop them—yes—you may be
right."

"You are thinking of the Beast Thing mutant?"

Jarl shrugged. "I think that he is a warning—there may
be other factors to set barriers in the way."

"I am mutant." For the second time Fors made that
bitter statement and he spoke it again before the one person he wished had never known of his difference.

Jarl did not rise to the bait. "I have been thinking that
we may all be mutants. Who is to say now that we are of
the same breed as the Old Ones? And I am of the belief
that it is time we all face that fact squarely. But this

other—this Beast Thing—" And he proceeded to drown
Fors in a barrage of questions which drew out of him all
that he had observed while a prisoner of the enemy.

Two days later the mountains stood sharply outlined
against the sky. Fors knew that by nightfall, if they kept
the pace they had held through the journey, they would
be past the outposts of the Eyrie. He fumbled awkwardly
with his one hand at his belt and pulled his sword from
the sheath. As Jarl caught up to him he held it out, hilt
first.

"Now I am your prisoner." He did not have to steady
his voice, it was naturally so. It was as if he no longer
cared what happened to him during the next few days.
This was a piece of unfinished living which must be completed before he left it behind him. But he was impatient
now to have it over, to be read out of the tribe as an outlaw, to go into the wilderness again—he was ready and
unafraid.

Jarl took his sword without a word and Fors glanced
beyond the Star Captain to the waiting Lura. She was tugging in his mind, suddenly weary of the leash of loyalty
which had held her to him through all these days of danger. She wanted the mountains, too, in a different way—
the mountains and her freedom. He gave it to her with a
single shaft of thought and she was gone that same instant. And because he had released her so willingly he
knew that she would return as willingly when she had followed her own desire to its end.

After that Fors rode in a kind of dream. He paid little
or no attention to the men of the Eyrie who came out of
their scout posts to greet the Star Captain. They did not
speak to him and he had no wish for them to do so. His
impatience to come to the judging only burned the stronger in him.

He was alone at last in the inner chamber of the Star
House, that same chamber which he had violated. The
empty hook where Langdon's star pouch had once hung

as a mute reminder of that offense. Too bad his venture
ad failed so completely. He would never be able now to
rove the truth of his father's dream. But even that
ought did not prick him overmuch. He could go out
gain—and not by any favor of the council men.

There was the reflection of the council fire on the
aked rock of the mountain wall out there. The elders
ere gathering to judge him. But it would be the Star
Men who would have the final voice against him. It was
e Star House he had looted, the Star tradition and mys-
ries he had flouted.

At an almost soundless footfall in the outer room Fors
urned his head. One of the Star Novices had come for
im—Stephen of the Hawk Clan. Fors followed him out
to the circle of firelight, walled in by rows of white blurs
hich were faces without expression.

The elders were together, all of them, Healer, Re-
order, Master of the Fields, Commanders of the Hunters
nd Defenders. And behind them were the tillers, the
unters, the scouts and guards. On the other side was the
olid block of Star Men, Jarl at their head.

Fors came out on the smooth shelf of rock alone, his
ilver head high, his back and shoulders straight.

"Fors of the Puma Clan—" That was Horsford, the
Eyrie Guardian.

"You stand here because you have defied the traditions
of the Eyrie. But against the wearers of the Star was your
greater offense. So now it is the decision of the Council
hat the Star Men shall be given the right to pronounce
against you and they shall deal with you as they see fit."

Short and to the point. And fair enough, he had expected little else. So now what did the Star Men wish for
him? It was up to Jarl. Fors turned to the tall Captain.

But Jarl was staring beyond him at the leaping flames.
And so did they wait in silence for a long, long moment.
When the Star Captain spoke it was not to pass sentence
but to catch the attention of all who gathered there.

"We come, men of the Eyrie, to a place where tw
roads separate before us. And upon our choice of ther
depends the future of not only the clans gathered here
but also that of all true men in this land, perhaps on th
earth. Therefore tonight I am breaking a solemn vow, th
oaths taken in my green youth—that secret which ha
made of my kind men apart. Listen, all of you, to the in
ner story of our Stars.

"Now we who wear them are hunters of dim trails
seekers of lost knowledge. But once this," his hand wer
to the star, bright and hot in the firelight, at his throat
"had another meaning. Our forefathers were brought t
this mountain hiding place because they were designed t
be truly men of the Stars. Here were they being trained t
a life which would be theirs on other worlds. Our record
tell us that man was on the eve of conquering space whe
his madness fell upon him and he reached again for slay
ing weapons.

"We who were meant to roam the stars go now on foo
upon a ravaged earth. But above us those other world
still hang, and still they beckon. And so is the promis
still given. If we make not the mistakes of the Old One
then shall we know in time more than the winds of th
earth and the trails of this earth. This is the secret w
now publish abroad so that all men may know what wa
lost to us with the dread folly of the Old Ones and t
what we may aspire if we make not the same error in ou
turn."

Fors' fingers clenched until nails bit into his palms. S
this was what man had thrown away! The same longin
which had torn him on the field of the dead bombin
plains came to him again. They had been so great in thei
dreams—the Old Ones! Well, men must dream again.

"We stand before two roads, my people," Jarl repeate
slowly. "And this time we must take a better choice. It i
the will of the Star Men that Fors of the Puma Clan
being of mixed blood and clan, shall no longer be held a

sser than we, in spite of the laws of our fathers. For
ow has come the time to break such laws.

"From this hour forth he shall be set apart in a differ-
nt fashion. For he shall be one who will carry the
nowledge of one people to another, binding together in
eace swords which might be raised in war.

"A mutant may have skills which will serve his tribe
ell. And so do we urge a new law—that a mutant be
eemed a full man. And if he is born in a clan, then is he
o be counted a man of that clan. Which of us can
rove—" Jarl swung around to face the throng from
hich was now arising a growing murmur, whether of as-
ent or dissent who could tell— "which of us can prove
hat we are of the same breed as the Old Ones? Do we
ish to be as the Old Ones? Our fathers threw away the
tars—remember that!"

It was the Healer who answered him. "By nature's
aws, if not man's, you speak the truth. It is guessed that
nen are different today from what they once were. A mu-
ant—" He coughed behind his hand. "Truly any here
night be termed mutant to some degree."

Horsford held up his hand to still the babble of sound.
His powerful voice boomed around the circle.

"There has been a weighty thing done here tonight,
orothers. The Star Men have broken faith with the past.
Can we do less? They speak of two roads— I shall speak
of growing. We have put our roots in narrow and stony
ground. We have held stubbornly to it. But now comes a
ime when we must move or die. For the only end to
growth is death. And in the name of the Council I am
choosing growth. If the stars were once promised us—
hen shall we reach for them again!"

Someone raised a cheer—it came from the outer edges
where the youths stood. And that cheer gathered voices
and grew. Men were on their feet now, their voices eager,
their eyes alight. Never had this reserved and too serious

people seemed so like their cousins of the Plains. The tribe was coming to a new life.

"So be it," Jarl's voice broke through the din. At his gesture of command some of it died away. "From this hour we shall walk new ways. And in remembrance of that choice do we now set upon Fors a star which is like unto no other worn here. And in his turn, when the time comes, he shall raise up those who will wear it after him. Thus there will be always those among us who shall speak with other peoples as a friend, think with neutral minds, and hold the peace of nations in their hands!"

Jarl came to Fors holding out a chain from which hung a star, not of five points but of many, so that it was a compass sign pointing in all directions at once. And this fell cool and smooth below the mutant's throat.

Then the tribe shouted the cry which was the welcome to a Star Man newly raised up. But in this too there was a difference. For now was born a new star and from it would follow what no man standing there that night might rightly foresee—not even he who wore it as a trust.